ONCE Was a TIME

Praise for *Once Was a Time*

A Junior Library Guild selection
A Parents' Choice Silver Honor

"Shines in its portrayal of friendship. Will appeal to fans of *When You Reach Me* and *A Wrinkle in Time*."—*School Library Journal*

"The bond between Lottie and Kitty . . . proves to be both tender and unstoppable."—*Booklist*

"Rewarding and uplifting."—*Kirkus Reviews*

"The real heart of this story lies in [Lottie's] friendship with Kitty."
—*Publishers Weekly*

"Will delight those who prefer to revel in the vast mysteries of time and coincidence."—*The Horn Book*

"*Once Was a Time* has it all: suspense, humor, an intrepid heroine, and an intriguing take on time travel. But at its heart, Leila Sales's dazzling tale is about a friendship so powerful that nothing—not even time itself—can break its bonds. Unforgettable."—Katherine Applegate, Newbery Medal–winning author of *The One and Only Ivan*

"At once epic and intimate, bold and gentle, and as boundary-breaking and timeless as the friendship that is at this story's magnificent heart. A gorgeous, exciting read."—Anne Ursu, author of the National Book Award–longlisted *The Real Boy*

"A timeless story of best friendship that is as original as it is authentic, as elegant as it is heart-wrenching. Sales is a master storyteller."
—Courtney Sheinmel, author of *Sincerely* and the Stella Batts series

ONCE Was a TIME

Leila Sales

chronicle books · san francisco

First Chronicle Books LLC paperback edition, published in 2017.
Originally published in hardcover in 2016 by Chronicle Books LLC.

ISBN 978-1-4521-6139-6

The Library of Congress has cataloged the original edition as follows:

Names: Sales, Leila, author.
Title: Once was a time / Leila Sales.
Description: San Francisco, CA : Chronicle Books, [2016] | Summary: In World War II England, ten-year-old Lottie is transported via a portal to present day Wisconsin, where she must find her way back to her family and her best friend, Kitty.
Identifiers: LCCN 2015030753 | ISBN 9781452140094
Subjects: LCSH: Time travel—Juvenile fiction. | Best friends—Juvenile fiction. | Friendship—Juvenile fiction. | World War, 1939-1945—England—Bristol—Juvenile fiction. | Wisconsin—Juvenile fiction. | CYAC: Time travel—Fiction. | Best friends—Fiction. | Friendship—Fiction. | World War, 1939-1945—England—Bristol—Fiction. | Wisconsin—Fiction.
Classification: LCC PZ7.S15215 On 2016 | DDC [Fic]—dc23 LC record available at http://lccn.loc.gov/2015030753

Manufactured in China.

Design by Kayla Ferriera.
Typeset in Tycho.

10 9 8 7 6 5 4 3 2 1

Chronicle Books LLC
680 Second Street
San Francisco, California 94107

Chronicle Books—we see things differently.
Become part of our community at www.chroniclekids.com.

To Rebecca Serle:
I would follow you across
time and space.

Part One

CHAPTER 1

Most people don't believe in time travel, but that doesn't mean they're right.

Kitty and I knew better. My dad had been telling us about time travel for as long as we could remember. The question wasn't whether it worked. The question was how.

Kitty was my best friend. She was exactly three months older and exactly two inches taller than me. And while my thick, dark hair fell halfway down my back like a curtain, Kitty's was light and blond and bouncy, like an angel's. Our eyes were the same, though—the sort of hazel that could look brown one day and green the next. Our eyes were so alike that they proved, we said, that we could have been sisters.

Kitty didn't have any real brothers or sisters, so her parents watched her constantly. That's why she came to my house whenever she could: so she could get away from them. And that's how she came to know as much about time travel as I did.

We were both fascinated by the idea of it. "Tell us again," we begged my dad over supper one Wednesday night. "Tell us again how it works."

"You know this is secret information," Dad warned us.

"We *know* that," I said.

"We would never tell anyone, Mr. Bromley," Kitty promised. "Even if they tortured us."

My little brother, Thomas, looked up from the story paper he was reading under the table. The word "torture" had caught his attention. "Even if they won't let you sleep for days and days?" he asked.

"Even then," Kitty said.

"Even if they stick needles in your eyeballs?" Thomas asked.

I shuddered.

"This is getting a bit too graphic for dinnertime," Dad intervened.

Thomas shrugged and returned his attention to *The Hotspur*. Unless conversation was specifically about war, Thomas wasn't interested.

"So there are portals," Dad said to me and Kitty, and we both leaned toward him, our Brussels sprouts forgotten on our plates. "They open up at random, and they exist only briefly. But if you step through a portal during the few seconds that it's open, you will be transported through time and space."

"What do portals look like?" Kitty asked, her eyes wide. Dad had described them to us loads of times, but Kitty and I wouldn't be satisfied until we had a photograph. Maybe not even then.

"Well, like doorways," Dad said, drawing one in the air with his hands. "Only shimmery and iridescent. They look like a ripply bit of air, if you can picture that."

I could picture it. I completely could. I knew exactly what I thought a portal looked like. I just didn't know if I was right.

"You've never actually *seen* one, though, have you?" demanded Justine, my fifteen-year-old sister.

"No," Dad acknowledged. "The vast majority of people will go their entire lives without ever seeing a portal. There just aren't that many portals, and they are so spread out across continents and centuries that the odds of encountering one are staggeringly small."

"So basically you could be making it up," Justine said.

Kitty and I glared at her.

"We don't have to see a portal to know that they're out there," Dad said. "Just like we don't have to see a molecule to know that the world is full of them, or see a supernova to know that they happen. The science supports it, and personally I trust science more than whatever I happen to glimpse through my own flawed eyes."

Kitty and I nodded our agreement, like scientists. Justine shrugged. "You've never even *met* a single person who's seen a portal," she said.

"Certainly I have," Dad objected. "You know this, Justine. I've told you all about the gentleman from Edinburgh who once found a portal in his parlor."

My sister scoffed. "And why ever did you believe him? I don't."

"Because," Dad said, "I interviewed him in detail, and his description of the portal, his knowledge of its shape and tenor—it was too dead-on to be faked."

"A coincidence," Justine suggested.

I knew exactly how Dad would respond to that. I reckoned Justine knew, too, and was just egging Dad on. And he said, as I'd expected, "When something seems like an unbelievable coincidence, then consider that it might not *be* a coincidence."

That was one of his favorite expressions.

"You're right to be dubious, Justine," Dad went on. "All great scientists doubt. That's why we become scientists. These are all just theories. Time travel is a theory. Gravity is a theory. Evolution is a theory. I suppose they might someday prove to be incorrect, but until then, they're the best explanations we have for the world around us."

"Super," Justine muttered, and she went back to reading *her* story paper under the table.

Everyone in my family read during dinner, and pretty much all the rest of the time, too. I had *A Little Princess* in my lap, and as soon as Dad finished telling us about time travel, I was planning to reread (for the eleventh time) the scene where Sara makes Miss Minchin cross by being secretly fluent in French. *A Little Princess* is my favorite book. I took it out of the library six times in a row before I had saved up enough pocket money to buy my own copy.

"Mr. Bromley, what will you do if someday you *do* see a portal?" Kitty asked.

"I'll study it, of course," Dad said.

"But would you go through it?" Kitty persisted.

I held my breath. I had never dared to ask him this question so directly, because I wasn't sure I could handle his answer. I wanted him to say no. I wanted him to say, *I would stay here with my family.*

He didn't. But he didn't say yes, either. "What you must understand, Kitty—"

"Catherine," she interrupted. Justine snorted and noisily turned a magazine page.

Kitty's real name was Catherine. When we first became friends, we were just babies in prams, and I couldn't pronounce "Catherine" yet. So I called her "Kitty," and it stuck. Now that we were ten, Kitty was worried that her nickname sounded too childish, so she wanted everyone to start calling her by her real name. "Plus," she had pointed out a few weeks ago, "'Catherine' has lots of good anagrams. You can rearrange the letters to 'Nice Heart.' Or 'The Race In.' You can't make *any* other words out of the letters in 'Kitty.'"

Kitty liked words whose letters could be rearranged to form new words. The better a word anagrammed, the more she liked it. I'd given her a book about anagrams last

Christmas, and already she seemed to be better at them than the book's author was. She kept finding ones that the book had missed.

She was right about her name, but I refused to start calling her Catherine anyway. There were two other Catherines in our form that year, but there was only one Kitty.

Dad went on answering her question. "What you must understand is that if you go through one of these portals, you have no idea where you're going to wind up. Or *when* you're going to wind up. You could find yourself in the twelfth century in the middle of the jungle. You could be transported to the center of the Atlantic Ocean in the year 2000. Wherever you go, odds are that it won't be safe."

"It isn't safe here, either," I whispered.

"Oh, we're perfectly safe, Lottie," Dad said.

And maybe he was right—my dad was usually right—but I didn't *feel* safe.

The war had been raging for more than a year now, and already I could hardly remember what life was like during peacetime. France had fallen to Hitler over the summer, and every day I worried that England would be next. On the wireless, Prime Minister Churchill said that we would never surrender—but how could he know that? The Luftwaffe—the German Air Force—seemed to be dropping bombs on London more nights than not. And even though we lived more than a hundred miles from London, the Luftwaffe had targeted Bristol, too. A few girls at my school had moved to the countryside for the duration; Alice Fitzhugh's parents had sent her all the way to Canada. Part of me wished I could escape with them, even though my dad said their families were being ridiculous.

Maybe the jungle in the year 1150 would be more dangerous. But then again, maybe it wouldn't be.

"The bigger problem with time traveling," Dad went on, "is not that you don't know where or when in time the portal will take you. The bigger problem is that you would *never* be able to find your way back home. The odds are infinitesimally small that you would see even one portal in your life, so the odds that you would then see *another* one are essentially impossible. And even if somehow, defying all odds, you did see a second portal, and you walked through it—well, it wouldn't take you home. It would take you to yet some other place and some other time."

Even Thomas and Justine were listening by now, though they were acting like they weren't. I could tell because they had stopped turning pages.

"So if you are ever given the opportunity to go through a portal," Dad said, "you had better be absolutely certain that you can handle never coming back."

I wondered what I would do if I somehow saw one, one day. I thought I would show it to my dad and let him decide what to do about it. I wouldn't go through it, I knew that. Certainly, my life in this time and place wasn't perfect. Hitler could conquer England any day, all my favorite foods were rationed, my sister made me cry on average once a week, and my teacher hated me because I was always reading under my desk during lessons.

No, my life wasn't perfect. But I wouldn't want to leave it behind forever. I liked my adventures to stay where they belonged: in books, where I could shut the cover on them any time I wanted.

"I would do it," Kitty announced, her eyes bright. "If I ever see a portal, I'll go."

"You're sure about that?" Dad asked with a smile.

Kitty nodded firmly. "It's like an unopened letter, isn't it? Even if you think there's bad news inside of it, how could you *not* be curious enough to open it?"

"What about me?" I demanded.

"What do you mean?" Kitty asked, her forehead crinkling.

"You'd go through a portal and never see me again?"

"Of course not, Lottie," Kitty said. "I would never, ever leave you. If I go through a portal someday, I'm taking you with me."

CHAPTER 2

When my mum left us, she didn't do it with shimmery portals and time travel. She did it the old-fashioned way: with a trunk and a train and a promise to write.

She left six months ago, in April. She went to stay with her sister in Highgate.

As I watched her pack, I asked, "Why would you leave Bristol, which is at least *maybe* safe, to move into the middle of London, which is definitely *not?*" I knew that people in London were doing whatever they could to get their children out of the city, away from the bombs, the frequent air raids, the closed schools. And yet here was my mum, running right in the opposite direction. "Are you *mad*, Mummy?"

"I'm not mad, sweetheart," Mum said, kissing the top of my head. "But I shall go mad if I stay here."

It's not you, she explained to Justine, Thomas, and me. But she didn't say that to Dad, because it *was* Dad. It was Dad and his obsession with discovering the secrets of time travel; that was the reason why she was leaving.

"Take us with you," I begged, but even as I said it, I knew I didn't mean it. I didn't want to live in London. I had been there a few times, to visit Aunt Matilda, and I found it dirty and crowded and loud—and that was *before* the war even began. I didn't really like my mother's sister, either: She always called me by my full name, Charlotte, even though I'd told her a hundred times that I preferred Lottie. And I didn't want to leave Daddy, either. What did it matter if he was obsessed with time travel? It was important. *He* was important.

Dad had signed the Official Secrets Act, so he wasn't allowed to tell us much about his time travel research, and this secrecy, I think, was part of what Mum couldn't stand. But Kitty and I paid attention, and we put things together.

We knew Dad's research at the university was funded by the government—by the British Armed Forces, specifically—

and we could guess that the plan was for him to work out how time travel operated, so that the military could harness it and create their own portals, which they would use for . . . something. Kitty thought they would go back in time to kill Hitler when he was just a baby. Stop the whole war before it even started.

If Dad could really do that—unlock the secret to time travel and thereby save all of Europe from this wretched war and its daily casualties—then there was no question in my mind that he should. That he *had* to. So what if he was in his laboratory all the time? Who could say that it wasn't worth it?

My mum, apparently. "I didn't sign on for being the wife of a mad scientist," we overheard her say to Dad the night before she left. "We" was me, Justine, and Kitty, who was spending the night at our house. We were listening outside their bedroom door. It was the only way to find out anything around here.

"Things will get better," we heard Dad promise.

"*When?*" she demanded.

"When the war ends."

"And when is that going to be?"

A moment of silence. Then Dad said, "When I find the answer."

Mum gave a little cry of frustration, and I pictured the two of them there on the other side of the door, standing across the room from each other like enemies on a battlefield.

"Do you have any idea how long I've wanted to have this conversation with you?" she asked. "But you haven't even been home enough for me to tell you that I'm leaving."

The three of us silently retreated to the bedroom Justine and I shared. Justine crawled under the covers immediately and clamped her pillow down over her ears. She didn't talk to me. Kitty was the one who held me as I cried, and Kitty was the one who told me it would be all right, and it was in Kitty's arms that I at last fell asleep.

It was now six months later, and we hadn't seen Mum once. But she did write, just as she promised. Every single week. And we wrote back, or at least Thomas and I did. Justine said she couldn't be bothered. I missed our mother terribly. Maybe Dad did, too, or maybe he didn't. I couldn't tell, because Mum was right about one thing: These days, he didn't seem to care about anything except his research.

In fact, he cared so much about his research that when he disappeared in October, I didn't even notice.

*　*　*

Kitty's family was different from mine. If Kitty's parents had gone missing for even twenty-four hours, we would have called the police. The McLaughlins always had a plan. They knew where they, and Kitty, were supposed to be at every moment of the day. If Mrs. McLaughlin nipped out to buy some milk, she would leave behind at least one note, sometimes more: *Gone to the High St. Home in 20 min. Bikkies on the table if you get hungry.* As if Kitty couldn't see that there were biscuits on the table next to the note.

It was because of the McLaughlins' obsession with always having a plan that Kitty and I had come up with one for what we would do if we ever got separated by the war. We'd heard stories on the wireless about families in occupied France or Poland who were suddenly ripped apart, some of them carted off to prison camps, others who simply disappeared in the middle of the night.

England was still proud and free, but if the Nazis ever occupied our country, too, Kitty felt firmly that she and

I should know how to find each other again. We'd come up with our plan just two weeks before my father's disappearance, on the night that Princess Elizabeth and Princess Margaret delivered their first-ever national address.

Kitty and I loved both the princesses, of course. We loved Elizabeth because she was going to be queen someday, but we loved Margaret more because she was almost exactly our age. I felt a special affinity for her because I, too, was a younger sister, and I wondered if Elizabeth ever teased Margaret in the way that Justine sometimes teased me. In photographs the princesses always looked calmly pleased to be in each other's company, but I reckoned that they argued when the cameras weren't there, just like any other sisters.

We dressed up in our princess costumes the evening we listened to their address on the wireless. We both wore paper crowns salvaged from last year's Christmas crackers, and Kitty carried a scepter (a fire poker) while I wore a long robe (my mum's).

"Don't the girls look so precious?" Mrs. McLaughlin asked her husband as she tuned in to the program for us.

"Darling," Kitty's father agreed, puffing on his pipe.

"*Regal*, Mum," Kitty corrected her. "We look *regal*."

I sat up straighter on my footstool. Straighter and more regal.

The princesses were speaking on *Children's Hour*, which we listened to most every evening for the stories, but this night was special. Kitty squirmed with excitement until finally the announcer said, "Her Royal Highness, Princess Elizabeth."

Her voice came through as clear as a bell, as if she was right there in the McLaughlins' front room with us. "In wishing you all 'good evening,' I feel that I am speaking to friends and companions who have shared with my sister and myself many a happy *Children's Hour*."

Kitty and I both started squealing.

"My word," remarked Kitty's mum, "if that isn't the poshest voice I ever heard come out of a child's mouth!"

"Naturally," Kitty said. "She's going to be the *queen*, after all." She adjusted her crown.

"Hush," I ordered them. "She's still speaking!"

"Thousands of you in this country have had to leave your home and be separated from your fathers and mothers," the princess continued. "My sister, Margaret Rose, and I feel so much for you, as we know from experience what it means to be away from those we love most of all."

I didn't even need to look at Kitty before I felt her hand close around mine. She squeezed it, and I squeezed back. I hadn't left my home, I hadn't gone anywhere at all, but I knew far too well what it meant to be apart from my loved ones.

"And when peace comes," the princess concluded, "remember it will be for us, the children of today, to make the world of tomorrow a better and happier place."

I wanted to do that, so badly: to make the world of tomorrow a better and happier place. And when I saw the determined look on Kitty's face as she stared at the wireless, I knew that she was vowing to do the exact same.

"Good night, children," said Princess Margaret.

"Good night, and good luck to you all," said Princess Elizabeth.

It was the best *Children's Hour* ever.

As soon as we turned off the radio, Kitty told me that we needed to come up with our plan to find each other if ever we were separated. It was as if hearing from the princesses had made her take this whole war business more seriously than ever she had done before. "We need to choose a meeting spot," she declared, gesturing authoritatively with her fire poker—I mean, royal scepter.

"You're right," I said. "What's the spot, then?"

"It ought to be somewhere we could find easily," Kitty mused. "And somewhere we know we'd be able to get into. Not our houses, for example. What if they took over our houses when they sent us away to prison camp?"

"Wills Tower," I suggested. Wills Memorial Tower was the grandest building at the university where my dad worked. Probably the grandest building in all of southwest England. It was made to look as if it had been built in medieval times, all vaulted ceilings and turrets raised toward the heavens. It reminded me more of a cathedral than a university.

Dad had taken me and Kitty to Wills Tower a number of times over the years. He had let us play hide-and-seek in the hallways and winding staircases while he sat in meetings. I knew we would be able to find it no matter what happened because it was right in the middle of Bristol, and it was one of the city's tallest buildings. You could see that tower from almost anywhere.

Kitty nodded her agreement, pleased. "Tell sir 'Wow!'" she added.

I blinked at her.

"It's an anagram of 'Wills Tower,'" Kitty explained. And that decided it.

That was how important it was, in Kitty's family, to always keep track of everyone's whereabouts.

I couldn't help but think how different my own family was. My dad often stayed at the labs so late into the night that we were asleep before he came home, and then went back there before we woke up the next morning. Some nights I don't know whether he came home at all. When that happened, Justine was supposedly "in charge," which meant that supper was cold fish and chips from the chip shop, and sometimes boys would come round to visit her. That's just how things were in my family these days.

So I wonder: Just how long did it take me to realize that Dad was missing?

CHAPTER 3

Perhaps I should have noticed my father's absence days earlier than I did. But in my defense, school had gone from bad to worse, and there wasn't room in my mind for anything else. What happened was this: Betsy, Margaret, and Jeanine had formed a club called the Film Stars, and they were inviting other girls in our form to join. And they weren't just walking up and saying, "Hey, do you fancy coming out to play with us at Margaret's this weekend?" No, there were formal invitations in fine handwriting on lovely stationery. And then if you accepted the offer of membership (which everyone did, of course), you got a Film Stars badge and a Film Stars membership card, and I even heard there was a Film Stars initiation ceremony, only none of the girls was allowed to tell what happened there because it was secret.

Let me be clear: The entire concept of the Film Stars was utterly soppy. All they did was go to the cinema together. That was it. And I could do that myself, without belonging to any sort of club. In fact I *did* do that myself. Often. With Kitty.

So I wouldn't have been upset not to find one of those formal invitations slipped into my desk, except that Betsy, Margaret, and Jeanine made it clear that they were *never* going to invite me.

"We don't want to hurt your feelings," Betsy said to me in the schoolyard one Friday morning in late October, "but we don't really think you would fit in. D'you know what I mean?"

"Sort of," I answered, clutching *A Little Princess* tighter against my chest.

"It's just that you read," Margaret added. "A lot. And that's not really what the Film Stars is about."

"I know," I said. "It's about films. I like films, too."

"Have you seen *The Wizard of Oz*?" Jeanine asked.

"No," I said. "But I've read the book."

They all nodded grimly, as if to say, *Exactly.*

"You know we're going to secondary school next year," Betsy explained. "So it's time we start acting a little more grown up."

I hadn't known that reading books was babyish.

"I can act more adult," I offered.

"It wouldn't really help, you know," Jeanine said in a fake-sweet voice. "The Film Stars just aren't looking for that whole 'girls with glasses' thing."

As if it was my fault that I needed glasses.

But still, it would have been all right, I could have dealt with it. Except that then they invited Kitty to be a Film Star.

Kitty and I sat down at our desks next to each other, and I saw her pull out the envelope, beautiful in lace and ribbons. She stuck it back in her desk really fast, as if she didn't want me to notice. But it was too late.

She didn't mention her Film Stars invitation to me the whole rest of the day, so I didn't bring it up either. She just acted like her normal Kitty self: splitting her lunch with me, distracting Miss Dickens just as she was about to shout at me (again) for reading during class, playing make-believe witches with me in the schoolyard. She behaved normally, but as soon as she got that invitation, nothing felt normal at all.

I slipped out of school as soon as the day ended, and I went home alone. From school to my house was a twenty-minute walk across the Downs, which is a vast, flat expanse of grass and basically nothing else for as far as the eye can see, except for a few barrage balloons, like Martian space-craft suspended high up in midair, which the Royal Air Force had installed when the war started. Sometimes we would come out here to fly kites, because there were no trees or buildings to block the wind.

This day was gray and blustery and rainy, like almost every day in Bristol. I didn't mind rain as a rule, but it was so much worse when it came whipping across the Downs at an almost horizontal angle, and the wind, finding no kites to support, dedicated itself to trying to knock me over. I had an umbrella, of course, but it wouldn't stand a chance against this wind, so I stuck it in my schoolbag and just let myself get soaked through. The cardboard box holding my gas mask banged painfully against my knees as I hurried forward. If Daddy was home, he would have a fire going and maybe a cup of Ovaltine and I would dry right up. If Daddy wasn't there, well, I could always use a towel.

"Hullo!" I shouted when I walked in the front door.

"What?" Justine shouted back from upstairs. Otherwise, no response. The downstairs was dark, and there was nothing in the fireplace but cinders.

Fine. I would make *myself* a cup of Ovaltine. Betsy said it was time to start acting more grown up. But what did she know about it? Being adult had nothing to do with watching more movies. Making your own Ovaltine when you were soaking wet and friendless because there was no one there to take care of you—*that* was grown up.

I went into the larder. No milk.

I started to cry then, so I suppose Betsy was right, and I really *am* a baby. Crying over spilt milk. Or no milk, really.

I huddled down on the kitchen's filthy tile floor, which hadn't been cleaned in weeks, maybe months, maybe even not since Mum left. I pressed my forehead against my sopping wet knees and wept. I was so noisy about it that I almost didn't hear the knocking on the front door.

Slow. Slow. Fast-fast-fast-fast-fast.

That was the pattern everyone in my family used to knock on doors: when Mum wanted to come in and tidy my bedroom, or when I wanted to bother Dad in his library. Kitty had adopted it, too, although her parents had no interest in secret knocking codes.

I stood up, wiped the back of my wrist across my eyes, and went to open the door. There I found Kitty, looking like a drowned cat. She had her book bag but no gas mask, a forgetful habit for which Miss Dickens frequently reprimanded her. "Thanks a lot for waiting for me," Kitty said.

I was so surprised to see her that I just stood there.

"Can I come in?" she asked. "I'm still getting rained on, you know."

I let her inside and went upstairs to get towels for both of us. We sat on the living room floor together, dampening the rug. "What are you doing here?" I asked.

"It's Friday," was her explanation. "Why wouldn't I be here?"

"What about the Film Stars?"

Kitty looked puzzled. "What about them?"

"They invited you," I said. "I saw their letter."

"Oh, right." Kitty shrugged, her towel bobbing up and down on her shoulders. "I said no thanks."

"Why?" I gasped. No one *ever* said "no thanks" to Margaret, Betsy, and Jeanine.

She wrinkled her nose. "Because I don't want to be a Film Star. Those girls are mean. And boring. And they didn't invite you. So it sounded like a stupid club."

I didn't say anything because the love that I felt for Kitty, which was always part of me, like background music to my life, suddenly crescendoed into a symphony so loud and powerful that I would not have been able to speak over it had I tried.

"Did you honestly think I was going to join a club without you?" Kitty asked, her eyes wide.

I shrugged.

"Lottie, are you *daft*?"

I nodded, and we both giggled.

"Come on," I said, standing up and heading to the mantel. "It's freezing in here."

So Kitty and I built a fire, together.

CHAPTER 4

Much, much later that night, Kitty and I were back in the living room. We'd spent hours designing a massive treasure hunt that went through every room in the house, and then forced Thomas to solve it. He got in a sulk when he reached the end and realized that there was no actual treasure to be found, so that was the end of that.

Then it was time for bed, but Justine kicked me and Kitty out of the bedroom for whispering and giggling too loudly, so now we were whispering and giggling too loudly downstairs, where my sister couldn't hear us. We were drinking Ovaltine that tasted more like sludge—a little bit of hot water with an awful lot of powder—and practicing our psychic connection.

My dad had told us about things called Zener cards that were used to test for extrasensory perception. A deck consisted of twenty-five cards: five showing a circle, five showing a plus sign, five showing three wavy lines, five showing a box, and five showing a star. If you were just guessing what the next card to come up would be, the odds were that you'd get about five of them correct. So if you got a lot *more* than that correct, then you weren't just guessing: You were exhibiting genuine psychic abilities.

Dad didn't think there was any scientific proof behind any of it, but Kitty and I really wanted to have a telepathic connection, so we made our own deck of Zener cards out of paper and practiced mentally beaming the pictures at each other. One time when Kitty looked at the cards and thought really, really hard about the image on each of them, I got *nine* correct. Justine told us it was just luck, but I could swear I'd seen the symbol appear in my mind's eye as if Kitty was broadcasting it directly to me.

Tonight we'd run through the deck a few times, but we hadn't done any better than eight out of twenty-five. Which was certainly better than average, but still not our personal best.

We were halfway through the deck, this time with me looking at the cards and trying to send the images to Kitty, when we heard a knocking sound.

"Daddy?" I called.

No reply.

It must have been the dying embers of our fire. I glanced at the windows to make sure the blackout curtains were drawn, so nobody outside would be able to see any light left from our hearth or the one lit lamp. That was a rule that Mum had been very strict about: If the Luftwaffe could see light, they would know where the cities were, and then they would know where to bomb. She'd put Thomas in charge of drawing the curtains half an hour after sunset every evening, and he took this wartime responsibility *very* seriously. If the air raid wardens could see light coming through the windows at night, they would yell and even fine you.

Of course the curtains were drawn tightly, like every night. Kitty and I went back to our cards.

"Squiggles," Kitty said.

It was a square.

"Square," Kitty said.

It was a circle.

"Star," Kitty said.

This one *was* a star. I smiled to myself and marked her answer on my score sheet.

Then the knocking sound came again, louder.

"I think there's someone at the door," Kitty said.

"Who would be knocking on the door this late at night?" But I was already on my feet and walking into the front hallway, Kitty right behind me.

I have a quick imagination. That's what my schoolteacher last year had told my parents, like she wasn't sure whether it was a good thing or a bad thing: *Charlotte has a quick imagination.* That meant that, in the few steps between the living room and the front door, I had already come up with a dozen possible explanations for the knocking—the odd knocking, which was not *slow. Slow. Fast-fast-fast-fast-fast.*

Maybe our neighbors had locked themselves out of their house again and needed to come in from the rain.

Maybe Justine had arranged a late-night rendezvous with one of her beaux.

Maybe Mum had realized her mistake in leaving us and had journeyed all through the day and into the night so she could come home. And had been gone so long that she'd forgotten the right way to knock.

But when I opened the door, the person standing there was not a neighbor, or a teenage boy, or my mum. It was a tall, slender stranger in a dark gray raincoat with a smart hat angled over her face. She looked like a film star. *Not* a Film Star, a real one.

"Hello, girls," she said, her voice calm but serious. "Which one of you is Charlotte?"

"I am." I raised my hand.

"Ah, so this must be your sister," the lady said, her eyes flickering over Kitty.

"Oh, yes," I said innocently. "That's why our eyes are the same color, you see?" We widened our matching hazel eyes up at her.

She gave a tense smile. "I do see. I'm afraid I need to discuss something serious with you, however. I have some news to share with you about your father."

"My father?" I repeated, and *that* was the moment when it occurred to me to wonder how long it had been since I'd last seen him. Today was Friday. I was certain I'd seen him on Tuesday. Hadn't I? Or had it been Monday?

"Yes," the film star woman said. "It's quite important. Would you come out to the car with me?"

Kitty and I peered past her, but in the rain and the dark, it was impossible to make out a car on the street. I ate a lot of carrots these days, even though I thought they tasted like medicine and dirt, because Mum said they would help us see better in the nighttime, but they didn't do anything for my vision right now. Every house on my street had its blackout curtains drawn, of course no streetlamps were lit, and any cars that might have been on the road were required to cover their headlights and taillights. Driving on a night like this seemed to be madness—how would you avoid running straight into a tree? Whatever had brought this woman to my house must have really been urgent.

"What is the news?" I asked, as politely as I could, because she was an adult, and she seemed important, and I didn't want her to tell Daddy that I'd been rude.

"It's not appropriate for me to tell you, unfortunately," she said with an apologetic smile. "Your father is in the car, and he would prefer to tell you himself."

Instinctively, I took a step out of my house, closer to the car. I was just in my pajamas, and the night air chilled me.

Kitty held back. "Who are you, though?" she asked, squinting her eyes. She was not trying as hard as I was to be polite.

The woman didn't look offended, though. She reached into her breast pocket and pulled out an identification card that she showed to me and Kitty. It had her photo on it and declared "Royal Department of Nuclear Research" at the top. "I'm with the government," she explained. "I've been working closely with Professor Bromley on his research into time travel portals."

I gave Kitty a look to say, *See? We can trust her.* Dad's research was secret. If this woman knew about it, she was safe.

"Can it wait until morning?" Kitty asked. She yawned elaborately. "We're *rather* tired."

"I'm afraid Professor Bromley would like to speak with you now," the woman said firmly.

My quick imagination was working at double time now. Was Daddy hurt? Had he heard that Mummy was hurt? Perhaps he had discovered the secret of time travel and needed to share it with me. Perhaps he needed my help.

I followed the woman through the spitting rain to the car, Kitty close behind me. A sleek black car came into view when we reached the street. The woman opened the door to the backseat, and Kitty and I both peered in. It was so dark that maybe I was missing something, but I couldn't make out a figure in there. I turned around. "Excuse me," I said. "Where—"

At that moment, two men emerged from the shadows. One grabbed me, the other grabbed Kitty. An instant later, he'd thrown a large burlap sack over my head, covering my entire body. After that, I saw nothing.

I yelled and wriggled and kicked, but a ten-year-old girl is no match for a fully grown man. A *strong* fully grown man. I kneed him in the stomach as hard as I could, but other than a quiet "Oof," he didn't even respond.

He picked me up and threw me into the car. I scrambled blindly for the door, but a second later, I felt the car accelerate away.

I'd been kidnapped.

I screamed as hard and as loud as I could, and I could hear Kitty screaming, too, which gave me comfort: Wherever they were taking me, at least they were taking Kitty, too.

I tried to shimmy out of the sack, but those men had tied it tightly at the bottom. I stuck my hand down there, hoping to loosen the knot, but all I succeeded in doing was falling out of the seat as the car suddenly turned a corner. I landed in a heap, my head knocking against Kitty's legs.

I stayed like that the rest of the drive, my head pressed to Kitty's shins, trying to convey through layers of skin and hair and burlap, *It will be all right. As long as we're together, it will be all right.*

Kitty started talking at some point. "We'll pay you," she offered to whomever might be listening. "Whatever you want, I promise our parents will pay. If you just let us go." Her voice wavered. "Please."

Nobody replied.

I didn't know if Kitty was right about her offer. Of course our parents would pay a ransom for us if they could, but I didn't know whether they could afford whatever these people asked for. Neither of our families were rich. Before the war, my dad was just a normal scientific researcher and physics professor at the university. We lived in a comfortable house, but it was nothing posh.

And this made me wonder: Why would they take *us*? There were certainly more profitable children available for kidnapping. I reckoned that Betsy would go for a higher ransom than Kitty and me combined—though whether her parents would want her back was another question entirely.

The car stopped some time later. Maybe after an hour, maybe longer. I wondered how our captors had gotten enough petrol to drive us so far away when it, like everything else these days, was strictly rationed. If they were really with the government, they could have accessed as much petrol as they needed—but if they were really with the government, then why were they kidnapping us?

I felt cool air rush in as someone opened the car door, and Kitty and I started screaming again in unison. Just in case anyone might hear us.

I was picked up again, slung over somebody's shoulder, and carried indoors somewhere. For a moment I couldn't hear Kitty anymore, and I panicked, becoming even more frenzied in my wrestling. "Kitty?" I screamed. *"Kitty!"*

"I'm here, Lottie!" she shouted back.

"Don't leave me!" I screamed. As if Kitty or I had any control over where we were being taken, or whether we would leave each other.

When the burlap sack was finally taken off, I found myself in a brightly lit, low-ceilinged room, empty except for me, Kitty, the tall woman, and the two burly men who had thrown us into the car. The room had no windows to the outdoors, no furniture, and no decoration. We could have been anywhere: Bristol, Bath, Cardiff, Reading, or a village so small it didn't even have a name.

Kitty immediately ran to the room's one door, but it was steel, and obviously locked—she tugged at the handle, leaning all her weight back, and nothing happened.

Have you ever had this experience, of being ten years old, and so small, and so powerless, that there's nothing you can do to help yourself? It's pathetic. It's humiliating. It's terrifying.

But I stopped paying attention to the locked door when I noticed what was on the far wall: a big window that showed another room. And on the other side of this window stood my father.

CHAPTER 5

"Daddy!" I screamed, running to the window.

My dad had always been half-bald, but his remaining hair now looked greasy, his face unshaven. I could see his mouth moving, but through the thick glass, I couldn't hear a word of it. I beat my fists against the glass. "Daddy! Help me! Dad! Daddy!"

I saw him start to cry.

Behind me, the tall woman in the raincoat spoke. "Professor Bromley," she said. "Good evening. I trust you have been well?"

I inhaled sharply. Because the woman's accent was unmistakable.

She was German.

How had I not noticed this back at the house? Of course she had been speaking in an English accent there, holding a British government ID card, but how had I not realized that all that was *fake*? Her German accent was obvious now, immediately frightening, especially to someone like me, who was so worried about the war that she thought every unexpected sound might be a bomber plane, and every foreigner was a German.

We had been kidnapped by Nazis.

But why? What would Kitty and I have to offer the enemy? Was this part of a new military technique? Bombing London, torturing spies, and kidnapping primary schoolers?

Kitty was next to me then, in front of the window. She grabbed my hand and we squeezed, holding on to each other for dear life.

"I am delighted that your daughters agreed to join us tonight," the German woman continued, her voice smug.

I desperately wished that I hadn't told this woman that Kitty was my sister. I had thought we were so cute. But if I'd just kept quiet, or told the truth, then maybe Kitty wouldn't be here right now. Maybe she would be getting the Home Guard to rescue us right at this moment. If these Nazis had been looking for Dad's children for some bizarre reason, that shouldn't have anything to do with Kitty.

"I'm not—" she began, but was cut off when one of the big men clapped a hand over her mouth.

"Professor Bromley," the German woman said, "I'm certain that you recall the terms of our agreement, but allow me to refresh your memory. Option one, you tell us now exactly how to create a time travel portal, and you, as well as your daughters, walk out of here free. That will be the end of all of this; you go home to your family.

"Option two, you continue to keep this secret, and you watch your daughters die. Right now."

On cue, the two men pulled handguns out of their waistbands and pointed them at me and Kitty. I gasped, and Kitty began to wail, her voice like an air raid siren in the background.

The woman pressed a button on the wall and said, "Why don't you give your answer to all of us, Professor Bromley?"

"Lottie!" Dad's voice came through a speaker as I watched his mouth move. "Are you all right, my love? Are you hurt?"

"I'm scared, Dad. Please help me. Please help."

He pressed his hands to the glass. "I'm so sorry this has happened, my darling. I'm—"

"Professor Bromley!" the woman snapped, her voice so German and so angry. "Will you give us the answer, or will you let your daughters die?"

"I don't have the answer yet," Dad said. "I've not worked it out. But please give me more time. I am close. I'm so close to a breakthrough. And then I will give it to you, all of it. Just let us go."

The German woman made a harsh sound in the back of her throat. "We have *given* you time, Professor Bromley. And frankly, we do not believe you. You have been the pre-eminent researcher on time travel for the past twenty years, and for the past two you have had all the government funding you could want—yet still you have found nothing? It stretches the limits of my imagination."

"Sometimes science works like that," Dad protested. "How long do you think it took humans to work out that the earth was round? How long were mechanics working on automobiles before they finally perfected them?"

"I don't care," the woman said. "I am not in the market for a new automobile. We have been patient, but we are done waiting for you to share your findings on your terms.

You will now share them on ours. So, what do you have to say for yourself?"

"I have given you all my findings already," Dad choked out. "I swear it. But if you give me a little more time, perhaps I can—"

The woman interrupted him. "Our scientists looked through your notes. Just a bunch of unproven hypotheses and unsolved equations. Give us your *real* findings, Professor Bromley."

"That's all there is." I watched Dad's lips tremble. "Perhaps . . . perhaps there is no such thing as time travel. Perhaps I've not found the answer because it doesn't exist."

I felt Kitty's hand squeeze mine even tighter, and I knew why. This was the first time we had *ever* heard my father suggest that time travel might be made-up. Every time Justine or Mum had suggested as much, we had scoffed, because *we knew better*.

No time travel? Then what was the point of any of this? If there was no time travel, Dad could have been a simple postmaster, like Kitty's father, and Mum could still be with us, and there would be milk in the larder, and Kitty and I would be asleep on the living room rug right now instead of trapped in a small room with guns pointed at our heads.

The German woman's eyes narrowed. "You mean to tell me that you have devoted your entire career and academic reputation, not to mention thousands of pounds in government resources, to studying something that *does not exist*?"

"I don't know!" Dad cried. "I just don't know yet. But if you give me a few more months—even weeks—perhaps I could find definitive proof either way. . . ."

The woman glanced at the men with the guns. They didn't say anything. They hadn't spoken once this entire night.

She turned back to my dad. "Professor Bromley, we do not believe you. We know you have this information, but to protect the interests of your country, you have elected not to share it with us. Very admirable of you, putting your daughters' lives on the line for Mother England, but very foolish. We will kill them now, and then we will continue to track down and kill every member of your family, every person whom you care about, until you reveal what you know."

The room was silent for a moment, except for the sounds of weeping: mine, Kitty's, and Dad's.

If this woman was correct, and Dad really did know the secrets of time travel but was just refusing to reveal them to the Nazis, then he was practically a war hero. He was willing to sacrifice anything it took to protect England, to keep the Nazis from winning. It was so brave, like the stories Kitty and I loved to listen to on the wireless.

The only problem was that one of the things he was willing to sacrifice was *me*.

I respected war heroes. But right now, I didn't want my father to be a hero. I wanted him to be my dad.

"Please . . ." Dad whispered.

And perhaps he said more, but I stopped listening. Because I saw something.

It was near the right side of the room, about three feet tall and two feet wide. It was flat, almost like a sheet of loose-leaf paper; a patch of air that looked a little bit iridescent, a little bit ripply, like a pool of water with oil spilt in it. Like a small, flat, ruffled curtain made of air.

In other words, it looked like a time travel portal.

Or at least, it looked like what I thought a time travel portal looked like. But of course I didn't *know*. Did anyone?

I tried to catch Dad's eye through the glass and get him to follow my gaze to the portal. But it didn't work; he was too busy staring at me, like he was trying to commit to memory the daughter he would never see again. And I realized that because the portal was flat, he wouldn't have been able to see it from his angle, anyway. It was possible that the only one who could see it was me.

Think, Lottie. Think.

What did I know about time travel portals?

"Professor Bromley, we will give you the count of five," the German woman said. "Then we shoot."

The two men cocked their guns.

"Five."

There are time travel portals. They open up at random, and they exist only briefly. But if you step through a portal during the few seconds that it's open, you will be transported through time and space.

"Four."

Kitty's fingers interlaced with my own, and her eyes found mine. Was there a way to tell her about the portal without saying anything? I tilted my head toward it and cast my gaze over to it and back again.

She looked. She didn't see. Wrong angle, again.

If you go through one of these portals, you have no idea where you're going to wind up. Or when you're going to wind up.

"Three."

I tugged at Kitty, but she stayed stock-still, like an animal caught in a trap. I tried with all my might to beam a thought at her, as if I was sending her another image from a Zener card. *Look, Kitty. Look. There's a portal there, look.* Never had I wished for something as hard as I wished in that moment for our telepathy to be real.

The bigger problem is not that you don't know where or when in time the portal will take you. The bigger problem is that you would never *be able to find your way back home.*

"Two."

"I love you," I whispered to Kitty.

"I will always love you," she whispered back.

If you are ever given the opportunity to go through a portal, you had better be absolutely certain that you can handle never coming back.

"One."

In that moment, I could have tried to pull Kitty with me. It might not have worked, but I could have tried.

Instead I dropped her hand and ran the few feet between me and the shimmery bit of air. I heard a scream behind me, and the crack of a bullet.

I jumped.

A whirling dizziness. A dazzling pain. Then, darkness.

CHAPTER 6

I was vomiting before I even opened my eyes. It hurt worse than anything: worse than the time I got sick from traveling on the train to London, worse than the time a couple of years ago when I ate undercooked meat and spent the next two days in the lavatory. It felt like my intestines were going to come spewing out of my mouth. Dad hadn't warned me about this part of time travel.

Because Dad had never done it. So he hadn't known.

When my retching finally slowed down, I inhaled a deep breath. Air. So I wasn't in the middle of the Atlantic Ocean.

That was something, at least.

I opened my eyes. I was lying on grass. It was hot.

That was as much as I could get right now.

I reminded myself that I was alive, and that this was a good thing. But it didn't feel like a good thing right then. It felt overwhelming. I curled my legs in toward my stomach and held on to them as tight as I could. I focused on breathing. Nothing more. Just breathing.

I lay still for a while as I waited for energy to seep back into my body. I was reminded of Aunt Matilda's old cat, Spots, who died last year. Spots had had seizures sometimes. They would come out of nowhere, making her thrash and jerk and foam at the mouth. Then she'd lie still. That meant the seizure was over. It would take Spots a long time to regain the ability to stand up and walk around. Aunt Matilda said she was "resolving herself."

That's what I was doing: resolving myself.

After a long while, I sat up, and immediately I turned to look for Kitty. But of course Kitty wasn't here. For the first time in my life, Kitty was nowhere to be found.

I could not think about that yet.

It was *very* hot. And sunny. Not a single cloud in the sky. A far cry from the dark night that I had left behind, and the rainy day before that. We almost never got sun like this in Bristol, and when we did everyone would run outside to play, because we didn't know how long the good weather would last.

I wondered whether I was still in England. I had never left England before.

The grass on which I sat seemed to belong to a big, blocky house made out of white wood. It didn't look like the buildings in Bristol, almost none of which had large, flat, unlandscaped lawns like this one.

I stood up. I left the house behind and headed for the road, which was wide and empty. I didn't see any automobiles. Had I traveled to a time before they existed? What came before that—hansom cabs? I didn't see any of those, either. I didn't see any signs of life. Though I did hear the chirping of birds. So at least *they* were alive.

All Dad had said about the limitations of time travel was that it wouldn't be possible to travel to a point in your own life that had already occurred. "Wouldn't that be peculiar?" he had said. "To have ten-year-old Lottie and thirty-year-old Lottie walking around at the same time!" So all I knew was that I had to be in a time before October 1930 or after October 1940.

In the grand scheme of the world's history, that didn't narrow it down much.

I looked up the road one way, then the other. They looked the same. So I picked one direction at random and started walking.

My plan was to find the High Street, find a newsagent, and use a newspaper to work out where and when I was. I had read books about time travel before, and that was what the characters always did.

Of course, I might be in a time before newspapers were invented. I didn't think so, though. The houses seemed well-constructed, and there were streetlamps with wires running overhead. This didn't look like a world before newspapers.

Or I could be in China. I wouldn't be able to read a Chinese newspaper.

So, this wasn't a perfect plan. But it was all I had.

I walked for a long time—close to an hour, I reckoned. But I didn't come to a High Street, and the sun just got hotter and hotter. I was sweating through my pretty pajamas that my mum had sewn for me. All the houses were so big and identical and spaced so far apart, I felt like I wasn't making any progress at all. A few cars drove past me, sleek and rounded and small. This must be the future. But none of the futuristic cars stopped for a ten-year-old girl in glasses.

I wanted to cry with frustration, but I hadn't drunk any water in hours, or possibly centuries, and it was so hot—I just didn't have any tears in me. It never happened like this in time-travel books. They always found newspapers immediately.

The next house had a swing in its lawn, and a boy who looked to be around my age was playing on it. He was wearing baggy trousers and a white undershirt with the words JUST DO IT printed on the front. I became suddenly self-conscious about my yellow pajamas. The top had a Peter Pan collar and puffed sleeves, which I thought was the height of fashion when I picked out the pattern, but it now occurred to me that perhaps I looked like a four-year-old. And I had grown in the months since my mum left, so the pajama bottoms reached only as far as my mid-calves. If I were this boy, I would have taken one look at the girl dressed in this outfit and said, "You are *definitely* a time traveler."

Still, I had to risk that. I didn't have much experience talking to strangers, or to boys, but so far my plan, such as it was, had been an utter failure, and I needed help.

"Hullo," I said, stepping onto his lawn and praying that he understood English.

"Hey," he said. He immediately jumped off the swing, his face turning a little bit red when he saw me. "What's up?"

"You're American," I blurted out.

The boy raised his eyebrows at me. "Yeah, I know."

All right. I had a country. The United States.

It was a start.

"Are you . . . British?" he asked, cocking his head to the side.

"I'm English," I replied.

"That's so cool," he said. "Like Harry Potter!"

He said "Harry Potter" in a terrible fake English accent. I looked at him blankly.

"Uh, never mind. My name's Jake."

"Pleased to meet you. I'm Charlotte Bromley." I stuck out my hand for him to shake, but he didn't seem to notice. Maybe they didn't shake hands in America in the future. "I was wondering," I went on. "Can you tell me how to get to the High Street?"

Jake looked puzzled. "I don't know where High Street is."

Bother. What a ridiculous country. How could you not have a High Street?

"Where is the nearest newsagent, then?" I asked.

"I dunno."

Maybe Jake just wasn't very bright. "Is there a place," I asked slowly, "where there are shops? And you could go buy, oh, let's say, some milk? And a newspaper?"

"Of course," he said.

Thank you, America. "How do I get there?"

"Um . . ." Jake ran his hand through his dark brown hair, making it spike up in spots. "I could ask my brother to give you a ride?"

"Oh, no," I said quickly. "I shouldn't want to be a bother. Just tell me which direction to walk."

"Walk?" He laughed. "No way. That'd take forever."

"Why?" I asked.

"Because . . ." He looked helpless. "It's far away from here. Look, let me just ask Noah. It's no big deal. All he's doing anyway is sitting around and playing Xbox."

I didn't know what Xbox was, but I also didn't have a lot of options. Jake seemed nice, and he was offering to help. Plus he was my age, and an American, so I trusted him. He didn't seem like he was going to suddenly turn into a Nazi spy.

Probably.

"Where do you live?" Jake called from the door to the house.

And it occurred to me that I had absolutely no way to answer that question. Nowhere. I lived nowhere.

If I told Jake, "I just time traveled from Bristol, England, in the year 1940," what would he do? Maybe my dad really *had* uncovered the secrets of time traveling, so maybe that would be a normal thing to say now. Maybe Jake would respond, "Oh, I time traveled to the year 1940 on holiday once. It was quite lovely." That would be brilliant. Because then I could simply travel home again.

But if time travel now was as much a mystery as it had been in 1940, then what would Jake's response be? I knew what Kitty or I would do if someone showed up on our doorstep and announced she was a time traveler. We would say, "That's super! Come inside and tell us all about it."

But I also knew that not everybody believed in time travel. And a normal person, a person who read fewer books than I and who had less of an imagination than Kitty—a person like the Film Stars, or like Justine—would laugh and call you mad.

I couldn't tell whether Jake was a normal person, but I did know that I needed his help. So I couldn't risk saying "I'm a time traveler" and having him call the insane asylum.

"I live," I said, "at Thirty Orchard Close." Because that was my real address. Which I might never see again.

Jake shrugged. "I don't know where that is. Anyway, let me grab Noah." He opened the door to his house.

"Could I . . ." I called, blushing with embarrassment. I didn't want to ask this strange boy. But I had to. "Could I also use your toilet?"

"Of course!" He opened the door wider, and I scampered after him. "Noah!" he shouted into the house. "Get your keys. We're going for a drive!"

CHAPTER 7

Jake's brother, Noah, was nearly seventeen. "He just got his license," Jake explained to me in a whisper as we piled into the car. "He's a terrible driver. But he probably won't kill us."

The way I saw it, I had already escaped death once today, so I might as well give it a second chance. Jake and I crowded into the backseat whilst Noah started the car. The driver's seat was on the opposite side from the cars I was accustomed to. Was that an American thing? Or a future thing?

Noah glanced back at us. "Why are you dressed like that?" he asked me.

My face felt hot and my Peter Pan collar scratched at my neck. If Kitty had been with me, I was sure she could have instantly come up with some explanation. But the only answer I could think of was, *Because I don't belong here.*

Fortunately, Jake came to my rescue. "Shut up, Noah. It's probably a costume or something."

I bobbed my head in agreement. Noah shrugged and turned back around to face front.

"I think it looks cool," Jake added, which I didn't understand, because I definitely felt *warm* in the still air of the car, not cool.

Noah snorted. "You would," he said to Jake. Then he touched something on his steering wheel, and angry, strange-sounding music started blasting all around us. It was too loud for conversation, which I was glad for. If the brothers asked me any more questions, I didn't know how I would answer them. I needed some sort of alibi, a fake identity. But without knowing more about the world I was in, I couldn't even begin to work out what that fake identity might be. Was the war still on? Had the Germans won? All wars must end at some point. Mustn't they?

Noah was the sort of boy Justine would have called "handsome," which is to say he was (a) male, and (b) within five years of her age. Had she been here, she would have been mercilessly flirting with him in the front seat.

But Justine wasn't here, and she never would be.

My stomach twisted at that thought. Had there been anything left in it, I might have been sick again, all over the seats in Noah's shiny round car. Yes, Justine was careless and judgmental and often lazy. But right now, I missed her so much.

And that was nothing compared to how I felt when I thought about Kitty. Kitty, holding my hand in her last moments of life. Kitty, promising to always love me. And me, diving through that portal. Leaving Kitty behind.

Why hadn't I at least *tried* to bring her into the future with me?

Because I was worried there wouldn't be enough time, and in our confusion and fear, the portal would close before we both made it there.

But even so, shouldn't I have died beside Kitty, instead of saving myself without her?

Why had I even insisted on going out to the car with that Nazi woman in the first place? Why had I told her that we were sisters? Kitty had sensed something was wrong with the whole situation. She had wanted to stay inside. I was the one who followed the scary woman, like a fool. Kitty had only followed me, like a friend.

And look where that got her.

I could not keep thinking about this. I had to think about the basics: figuring out what year I was in, and finding a safe place to sleep tonight. If I thought about Kitty, I would shatter into a thousand splintered pieces, and I would never be able to put myself together again.

It was a fifteen-minute drive to the High Street, back in the direction that I had first come from. I could see why Jake told me not to walk. The dashboard in the car gave the temperature as 92 degrees Fahrenheit. I didn't think the weather in Bristol had ever been that hot.

Inside the car, though, cool air blew on us from vents in the ceiling. I wanted to ask how they worked, but I kept my mouth shut.

Noah screeched to a stop and turned off the car. I got out and felt the sun immediately beating down on me again.

"Is this what you were looking for?" Jake asked.

I looked around the street. I saw what looked to be a grocery shop, a bank, a post office, a few other shops, and a library.

A library!

For the first time since the Germans showed up at my house, I smiled. "Yes," I said. "This is exactly what I was looking for. Thanks ever so much."

"Are you guys going to be here for a long time?" Noah asked.

Jake looked at me, so I supposed Noah was speaking to both of us, even though I was obviously not a "guy."

"I should like to go to the library," I said.

It took Jake a moment to reply, and it occurred to me that maybe the Film Stars were right, and really nobody did like girls who read books. Maybe in the future, reading all the time was an even worse crime than it had been at Westminster School for Girls.

But then Jake just said, "Cool. Me, too. Meet us there in like half an hour, Noah?"

"Whatever," Noah said, which I decided must be Future American for "yes."

Jake and I went into the library, which was strangely chilly, just like the car. But other than that, and a few objects that I didn't recognize, it looked like the Bristol library. Scattered lamps and desks, a few comfortable-looking armchairs, and row after row of books. It even smelled the same as my library, the musty odor of paper that I loved more than any perfume.

I stood in the entryway for a moment, just breathing in. In this strange country, in this strange time, I felt at home.

"I'm going to the children's room," Jake whispered to me. "See you in a bit?" I nodded, and he took off.

"Excuse me," I said to the librarian with a short haircut at the front desk, "have you got today's newspaper?"

"Of course," she said.

Thank you again, America. This is a civilized land after all.

"Which paper do you want?" she asked, adjusting one of her dangling earrings.

I stared at her blankly. "The local newspaper," I said at last, hoping that was a legitimate answer.

Apparently it was, because she handed me a newspaper attached to a wooden post. "You can't check it out," she said, "but you're welcome to read it as long as you're in the library." I started to head to one of the comfortable-looking armchairs, but then she added, "I'm sure you get this all the time, hon, but I have to say, your accent is *adorable*."

"It is?"

"British, right?"

"It's English," I corrected her.

"I love British accents. I'm totally addicted to the BBC. It's my favorite television channel."

"You have the BBC?" I gasped. Last year, the BBC Television Service had stopped broadcasting "for the duration of the conflict." If the BBC was back on the telly, did that mean that Britain had won the war? And why would they get the British Broadcasting Corporation in America?

"Of course! Anyway, there's something about British accents that's so charming and old-fashioned, you know? Especially yours."

That's because I am old-fashioned.

"And . . . what an outfit, too," the librarian added, looking confusedly at my pajamas.

Thanks to Jake, I was ready for that one. "It's a costume," I told her. Then I walked away and sat down with my newspaper. It was called the *Sutton Telegraph*. After reading some of the fine print, I deduced that Sutton was a town in the state of Wisconsin. My United States geography was not very good, so I didn't know what that meant.

I found the date on the very first page. August 20, 2013.

Seventy-three years had passed. I was on a different day, in a different month, in a different year, in a different decade, in a different century, in a different *millennium.*

Which meant that everyone I knew was probably dead. If my dad had lived through being held captive by the Nazis, he would now be one hundred and eighteen. If my mum had lived through the bombings in London, she would now be one hundred and eight. If Betsy, Margaret, and Jeanine were still alive, they would be old women, ugly and wrinkled and, with any luck, too nearsighted to watch films.

Not that I am vengeful.

Now that I knew where and when I was, I had to work out where and when I was going. I didn't have a plan for that. I was simply exhausted.

I went to find Jake in a side room that was small and cozy, but absolutely jam-packed with books. I had never seen so many books just for children!

"Are you ready to go?" Jake asked, casting aside the colorful comic he was reading.

"I should like to stay here," I answered. "But you can go."

Jake looked dubious. "How will you get home?"

"I'll ring my mum and ask her to get me," I replied. "I'll be fine."

"The library closes pretty soon," Jake said. "Are you sure you don't want a ride? Noah would be happy to drive you pretty much anywhere. Trust me. No distance is too far for him."

"I'll be fine," I repeated, more curtly this time.

"Right. Okay. I get it." Jake ran his hand through his hair again. "I guess I'll see you around then, Charlotte."

He left, and it was just me and the books. So many books! I picked one up and flipped to the copyright page. It was published in 1999! I was holding in my hand a book from the future. Or the past, depending on how you looked at it. Either way, I had loads of missed books to make up for, and I had no idea where to begin.

I decided to go alphabetically, just so I wouldn't get overwhelmed. I picked up a book with a picture of a feather on the cover, by an author whose last name was Almond, and I took it to the armchair in the corner of the room. I curled up into the smallest little ball I could manage, and I read about a boy who found in his garage a man who was both bird and angel. I stayed there through announcements about how the library was closing, through the dimming of the overhead lights, through the sound of the librarian clicking the front door locked behind her.

In that armchair, hidden away in the far corner of the children's room, I fell asleep for the first time in seventy-three years. And all night long, I dreamt of Kitty.

CHAPTER 8

I awoke with a start, my neck aching from the awkward position I'd slept in.

Where was I?

The library. The future. Of course.

I checked the wall clock. It was just past nine in the morning. Light was streaming in through the windows, while inside everything was still quiet, the library obviously not yet open.

I rolled my tongue around in my mouth, trying to get rid of the dryness. I hadn't brushed my teeth or eaten since being sick yesterday, and the taste of vomit lingered.

I stood up, stretched, and tried to deal with my situation as best I could. First I found a lavatory. I drank straight from the tap for a couple of minutes, the cool water sliding down my throat. I took more water and splashed it on my face, and worked some through my hair, trying in vain to tear through all the tangles. It wasn't a bath. But it was a start.

My stomach rumbled, so I left the lavatory and went on a hunt through the library for something to eat. I didn't really expect to find anything, since food was distinctly Not Allowed at the Bristol library, and I couldn't imagine that rule had changed over the past seventy-three years. But I couldn't go out and buy anything, since I didn't have money or a ration book on me—and even if I had, it would have been English coins, not whatever sort of currency they used here in America.

Behind the librarian's desk, I found a bag of individually wrapped chocolates and another bag of small crackers shaped like fish. I tucked in as if I hadn't eaten in years. I devoured as many goldfish as I thought I could get away with, and I sent out a silent apology to the nice librarian with the short haircut whose food I was probably stealing.

Now that I was clean and full—sort of—I felt much more optimistic about things. A library wasn't the worst place to live. It had cozy chairs and running water, and I knew that I would never get bored here. Feeding myself regularly was going to be the big problem, but I would work it out. After all, I had read *A Little Princess*. Sara Crewe was an orphan, too, and she had survived in far worse conditions than mine. Maybe I would even get a rat to be my friend, as Sara had. This idea repulsed me: Rats scared me, the disgusting way they scurried around. But Sara had found that a rat friend was better than no friends at all, and perhaps I would find the same.

I wanted to sit back down in my armchair and finish reading the book about the bird-angel-man, but I knew the librarian would return at some point, and I didn't want her to find me and start asking questions about exactly how I got into the library before it was open for the day. So I got that book, as well as the one that came next, alphabetically—the author's last name was Applegate—and I squeezed into an empty bottom shelf of a bookcase in the back of the nonfiction room. It was the perfect hiding spot. Someone would only find me if she turned on the lights, got down on the ground, and looked.

Mummy always used to yell at me for reading without turning on a lamp. "You'll ruin your eyes!" she would threaten.

"My eyes are *already* ruined," I'd remind her, pointing to my glasses.

But Mum wasn't here, and she never would be. So if I wanted to read in the shadows of a bookcase in the corner of a darkened library, I could.

This is a game, I told myself. Like the sort of games Kitty and I used to play. *If you could play then, you can play now.*

A few hours later, after the overhead lights had been turned on and I started hearing different voices throughout the library, I decided there were enough people in the building that nobody would notice one more. I uncurled myself from my hiding spot, my cramped legs buckling under me.

An older man, standing at the end of the row, turned to gawp at me. My heart started pounding. "Sorry," I squeaked out. "I was . . . playing hide-and-seek. Yes. Well, all right, then. Good-bye!"

I gave him an "I'm a harmless child" smile and fled as quickly as I could.

The nice librarian was at the front desk, and she waved when she saw me. I was briefly concerned that she'd ask something like, "When did *you* walk in that door?" but all she said was, "It's my British friend from yesterday! Good to see you again."

The librarian looked to be somewhat younger than my mum, maybe in her early thirties. Today she was wearing a pretty navy-blue skirt that ballooned around her knees and a polka-dot headscarf. She didn't look anything like the Bristol librarians, who were all old ladies with prunelike faces whose vocabulary consisted entirely of the word "Shh!"

"Same costume today, I see," the librarian said, pointing at my pajamas. Goodness, was I growing weary of my pajamas. "I feel you," she went on. "When I was a kid, I went through a phase where I dressed up as Miss Piggy every day for two weeks. I refused to wear anything else. My parents would have to take the dress off me while I was asleep, wash it, and put it back on before I woke up. Can you imagine?"

I didn't know who Miss Piggy was, but I nodded as if to say, "Me, too. I have parents here who do that, too."

"My name is Jennifer Timms, by the way," the librarian said. I searched my brain for anagrams of *Jennifer Timms*, but I'd never been as quick at it as Kitty was, and nothing came to me.

I did not want to introduce myself to this lady, did not want to make any sort of strong impression on her. I didn't want her to remember that she kept seeing me here, day in and day out. But it seemed like it was already too late for that. So I said, "I'm Charlotte Bromley," since my mum always introduced me with my full name. I stuck my hand out. Unlike Jake, Miss Timms shook it. Apparently some Americans knew what that meant, after all.

"Can I help you find something today?" Miss Timms asked. "Another newspaper?"

And I didn't want her help, didn't want her to know or notice too much about me . . . but she might have the answers I needed. I tugged at my hair and peered up at her. "My father once told me, 'A librarian can work out the answer to any question.' Do you think that's true?"

Miss Timms tapped her pen against her teeth, and I liked that she paused, because it meant she was taking me seriously. "I guess it depends on the question," she said at last. "But I'd say that with enough time, a good librarian can work out the answer to *almost* any question."

"Then can you help me work out what happened to some people who lived in England a long time ago?" I asked, blinking rapidly. "In the 1940s, for example?"

I needed to know what had happened to them. All of them. Mum and Dad and Justine and Thomas . . . but most of all, more than anything, Kitty.

Of course the Nazis had shot her. I'd left her with a gun pointed at her head and not a second to spare. Kitty died that night—she must have—and I knew it because I was there. But I hadn't seen her body, and I wouldn't believe it until I had proof.

Anyone would grasp at straws if straws were all that was left.

"I think we could probably figure that out," Miss Timms said. She didn't ask why I was looking for this information, and this was one of the things that I had always appreciated about librarians: They didn't ask why. If you wanted a book about stinging nettles, they didn't say, as Mum might, "Oh my goodness, did some nettles sting you?" If you wanted a book about romance and heartbreak, they didn't say, as Justine might, "Why, do you *fancy* someone?" Librarians just liked to share information, and they didn't need to know why you wanted it.

"Do you want to find out about specific people," Miss Timms asked, "or just generally about what life was like in the 1940s?"

"Specific people," I said. I already knew what life was like in the 1940s.

She paused for a moment, and I could almost see the wheels in her head turning, whirring, sorting thoughts. "There's a database of obituaries you can use," she said at last.

"Obituaries," I repeated. "Those are what they write about people . . . when they die."

"Right. Here, follow me, and I'll show you how to use the database."

I had no idea what a database was, but I followed her nonetheless. Miss Timms led me past bookcase after bookcase to a group of small tables, each of which had on it a metal device, like a thin rectangular board.

"You can sit," she offered, so I took a seat in front of one of the flat boards and wondered what this metallic object would have to tell me about Kitty McLaughlin.

"Why don't you open up a browser," Miss Timms said to me. "The database is online."

I had absolutely no idea what she was talking about. I stared at her. I stared at the thin board. I waited for something to happen. Maybe an envelope would appear that said "browser" on it, so I could open it.

A minute went by, then another.

"Charlotte," Miss Timms said finally, "do you not know how to use the Internet?"

I shook my head and felt myself blush a little, because, even though I hadn't a clue what the Internet was, I could tell from Miss Timms's tone that this was something I was supposed to know.

To her credit, she did not say anything like, "What year did *you* travel here from?" even though it seemed as if maybe she wanted to. Instead, she just pulled up another chair to sit next to me and said, "Hon, get ready, because I am about to show you something that will blow your mind."

Chapter 9

Half an hour later, I knew how to use the Internet. Well, a little bit. I knew how to search a database of obituaries to find out about any person who had died since the year 1858. Miss Timms said there was more to the Internet than that, but she couldn't teach it all to me in one sitting. "Come back tomorrow," she said, "and I'll show you how to use e-mail." Then she left me alone with the obituary database so she could help someone else. I didn't explain that I wouldn't have to *come back* tomorrow, since I would already *be here*. I did want to learn more about the Internet, though. It seemed to have *everything*. Every answer in the whole world. And I wanted answers so badly, because right now, I had only questions.

Who to look up first?

I decided to go with someone who I didn't know personally. That seemed easier than reading about someone
who I knew and loved.

So, naturally, I started with Hitler.

*Adolf Hitler (born April 20, 1889) was an Austrian-
born German politician and the leader of the National
Socialist German Workers Party. He was chancellor
of Germany from 1933 to 1945 and dictator of Nazi
Germany from 1934 to 1945. He was the author of an
autobiography,* Mein Kampf, *one of the founding texts
of the Nazi Party. Shortly before Germany lost World
War II, Hitler married his mistress, Eva Braun, and the
couple committed suicide on April 30, 1945, to avoid cap-
ture by the Red Army.*

The obituary went on and on—Hitler was a famous man,
so there was a lot to say about his life, the Holocaust, the
war he started that killed millions of people. But I stopped
reading there, because I had already learned all I needed to
know. Hitler died. And Germany lost.

That was good news, and it filled me with relief. But
it filled me with sadness as well. I wasn't sad that Hitler's

army had lost, of course. But I was sad that he had been born in the first place, sad that he had been the ruler of Germany and that the war had happened, just as I remembered.

I had wanted to believe that ultimately, somehow, my dad *did* unlock the secrets of time travel. That all of it—Mum's leaving us, Dad's long hours at the labs, the kidnapping, my jumping through time—had paid off. But if Hitler existed and did all those terrible things, then nobody had traveled back in time to kill him, and my dad was just another failure.

I wanted to run home to tell Thomas, "We won the war! We won!" Then I remembered that my brother, if he had lived to see 1945, would already have known that.

I hoped he had lived to see the war end. He would have enjoyed that.

So I looked up his name next. There were a lot of Thomas Bromleys, but when I narrowed it down to the year and place of my brother's birth, there was only one.

Thomas Bromley (born in Bristol on February 2, 1933) was a political commentator for the BBC. He lived most of his life in London. He died on July 8, 1997, from a massive coronary. He is survived by his wife, Denise, and his sons, Michael and Paul.

My baby brother, a political commentator for the BBC? That was absurd. I tried to picture him as a grown-up news reporter, but all I could imagine was seven-year-old Thomas with his model airplanes, screeching, "It's a fighter plane! Pow, pow! She's going down!"

How could that vibrant, energetic boy have lived his whole life, moved to London, had children of his own, and died, when I had just seen him yesterday? It wasn't right, it wasn't *fair*, for me to have missed all of that. I was his big sister. I was supposed to watch out for him.

I briefly considered looking up Denise, Michael, and Paul—these people whose Christian names I did not recognize, but whose surname was my own. At least one of them was bound to still be alive. Maybe Michael or Paul would want to adopt their father's sister.

But had Thomas told them about time travel? Did they know I was alive? Could the news of my time travel have made it out of that locked room if Dad and Kitty were never set free?

I tried Justine next. If she were still alive, she would certainly give me a home. I wouldn't give her a choice.

Justine Liu (née Justine Bromley, born in Bristol on March 16, 1925) was a devoted gardener and a patron of the arts. After marrying Albert Liu in 1956, the couple eventually settled in Mr. Liu's native Taiwan, where they amassed a sizable collection of Oriental art. Justine Liu died on December 5, 2012. She is survived by her husband and her daughter, Grace Young.

That snapped at me, like a quick jab to my stomach. Justine had died in 2012. It was now 2013. I had come *so close* to seeing my sister again, seeing Taiwan (Taiwan!), seeing her sizable collection of Oriental art (when did Justine start liking Oriental art?). If only the portal had sent me one year earlier . . .

Time, it occurred to me then, was not very fair.

Mum's obituary next. I felt my breath coming fast, as if I'd been running too quickly, and I hugged my arms around my middle to stop my body from shaking. It's not easy to read about how everyone you know died, all in one sitting. I wanted to stop so badly. I wanted to go back to reading a story.

But walking away from this computer wouldn't bring anybody back. Their obituaries would still be here, whether I read them or not.

Elizabeth Bromley (née Elizabeth Smith, born in Bristol on May 14, 1904) accomplished many things in her eighty-six-year life; she was the mother of three children, the wife of scientist Robert Bromley, an ambulance driver in London during World War II, an accomplished soprano with the Christchurch Ladies Choir, and a professional reader of books for the blind during the last thirty years of her life. She died on July 5, 1990. She is survived by her children, Justine Liu and Thomas Bromley.

She was not survived, I noticed, by *me*.

Still, Mum had lived through the war. She had lived a good, long life; she had not been hit by a stray bomb on the streets of London. And that should be a relief.

Should be, but wasn't really. A relief would have been to see Mum again, to be held in her arms, to smell her perfume. To at least have known, that day when she left for London, that this was not just good-bye but our *final* good-bye, that I would never have another chance to see her face.

Out of all the obituaries I had read so far, it was Mum's that shocked me most. I'd not known that my brother would become a political commentator, or that my sister would move to the Orient—but they were young when I knew them, with their whole lives ahead of them. Of course I'd had no way of knowing what they would become. I was only ten; maybe someday I would move to the Orient, too.

But my mum, when I knew her, was a *grown-up*. She was old. How had she had this whole secret life that I'd never known? My mother, an accomplished soprano? I didn't know she sang at all, except for sometimes quietly, to herself, while washing up. And she read books for the blind? As a job? Mum had never held a job before.

I didn't know she had been driving ambulances in London, either. I thought she moved to London just to live with her sister and do . . . well, nothing, I suppose. An ambulance driver! That was so brave. That was so dangerous. I felt proud as I read that sentence. But I was also confused, and sad, to think that there had been so much to my mother, and now I would never get to discover it all. How peculiar to realize, more than seven decades later, that Mum had been doing *her* part for the war effort, just as Dad had been doing his.

Thinking of Daddy reminded me, as if I could have forgotten, that I needed to look up his obituary, too. What had happened to him? He saw me travel through time right before his eyes. He saw me dive through a shimmery screen of air and never return.

And then what?

I couldn't stop my teeth from chattering, and my hands felt numb. I didn't know how Americans did it, this artificial cooling, but it was too much. I wished it would stop, even for a moment. It was so cold in this library.

Robert Bromley (born in Pangbourne on July 24, 1894) was the Duncan Henley Endowed Chair of Physics at Bristol University. He was a dynamic, inspired lecturer, whose laboratory research focused primarily on electrical and magnetic properties of light. He died on October 25, 1940, in a blackout incident. He is survived by his wife, Elizabeth, and his children Justine and Thomas.

I leaned back in the desk chair. October 25, 1940, was the day that Kitty and I had been kidnapped. It was the last day that I saw my dad. And, apparently, the last day that he was alive.

A "blackout incident"? What did that mean? "Blackout incident" wasn't how *I* would describe getting captured by Nazis with guns. Furthermore, this obituary didn't say anything about Dad's *real* work—which made sense, perhaps, since it was so secret. Not once had I ever heard Dad say anything about "electrical and magnetic properties of light." That wasn't his research. His research was time travel.

When I read Mum's obituary, I felt uncomfortably as if this nameless, faceless obituary writer somehow knew my own mother much better than I ever would. But when I read Dad's, I sensed that the writer did not know him *at all.* And that feeling was even worse.

I kept staring at the computer screen as though it might suddenly tell me something more about my father. Something real, something that would make sense. Dad had always been able to explain things, whether it was time travel or the mean girls at school or the way kites flew across the Downs. That was just how his brain worked.

But from beyond the grave, my dad explained nothing, and nothing made sense.

I felt like my heart might break. I could not bear all this loss, all at once.

I wondered whether there was an obituary for me, too. Did people think I had died? How else would they explain someone who simply ceased to exist? So I searched. It wasn't hard to find.

Charlotte Bromley (born in Bristol on October 18, 1930) was the daughter of Robert and Elizabeth Bromley and sister of Justine and Thomas. She had a great imagination and she loved books. She died on October 25, 1940, in a blackout incident.

So that was me, then. That was all there was to me. I felt so disconnected from this girl described on the computer. Yes, that was my name, and yes, that was my birthday, and yes, I loved books—but that girl was dead. And yet, here I was.

I wanted to stop there, to walk away from the computer and lose myself in somebody else's fiction. But I forced myself to keep going, to type in Kitty's name.

It took me a long time. It was hard to find the right keys. They didn't go in alphabetical order. My dad had a typewriter, but I never used it, so I wasn't sure whether or not its keys were in the same order as these.

When I finally managed to type in "Kitty McLaughlin," the database turned up no results. My heart soared. Kitty was alive! *Kitty was alive!* There was no obituary, so she had not died!

Then it occurred to me, like a hand clenching around my neck, that she might be in there by her full name. The one I had never called her, the one with all the pretty anagrams. And when I typed in "Catherine McLaughlin," there she was.

Catherine McLaughlin (born in Bristol on July 18, 1930) was the daughter of Harriet and Brendan McLaughlin. She was a good student, and she enjoyed word games and swimming. She died in a blackout incident on October 25, 1940.

My eyes felt hot and my head hurt. *She was a good student, and she enjoyed word games and swimming.* What utter tosh. What a ridiculous thing to say about a life, a person—especially when that person was Kitty, who was so much more. This obituary could go on for pages, chapters—forever—and it would never do justice to the person Kitty was.

But I suppose that's what happens when you die at the age of ten. You will never chair a university department, or marry, or collect Oriental art, or sing in the Christchurch Ladies Choir. You will be remembered as a good student who enjoyed word games and swimming, because there wasn't time for you to show the world that you were anything more.

For minutes, maybe hours, I sat huddled at the computer in the library in the artificial cold. There was nothing left to hope for now. That computer knew the truth, and now so did I:

Kitty was gone. I had time traveled to safety, and I had left my best friend behind to die.

CHAPTER 10

What do you do when you learn, without a doubt, that you've lost everyone you love and you're trapped by time forever?

I didn't know. So I just read another book. And I anagrammed things. The "Read a book!" poster on the wall became "a bake odor." The name of the author of the bird-angel-man book became "diva and mold." Nothing I came up with was particularly impressive, and Kitty could have done much better, but at least focusing on words took my mind off my real life for a little while.

After a few hours, I felt like I should eat, even though I couldn't imagine ever being hungry again. I left the library in search of food. It was still hot outside, and I felt like I was wilting under the sun as soon as my feet hit the pavement. I thought maybe I could pick nuts and berries, or possibly kill a rabbit, like in the wilderness survival books I'd read. But I didn't see any bushes that looked like the nut or berry type. Nor did I see any rabbits. Nor would I have had any idea how to kill a rabbit, had one suddenly appeared. Instead I pulled a half-eaten sandwich out of a rubbish bin on the corner, and I ate that. It made me feel wretched, but I supposed I deserved to feel wretched.

Shortly before six o'clock, when the library was due to close, I slipped back inside and hid once again in the bottom shelf of the bookcase. I came out only once I was certain Miss Timms was gone.

I'd fantasized before about running away to live in a library. All the books I could ever want, right there in my home—what could be better? But in my fantasies, I'd always packed money and food and a toothbrush. In my fantasies, Kitty had always come with me.

I thought about all the stories I'd read about orphans and runaways. Sometimes they slept in abandoned buildings, and sometimes they slept in train cars, but always, at the end, they found a family. Children never stayed on their own forever.

How long could I keep this up?

The answer was: Not much longer at all. Because when Miss Timms arrived at the library the next morning, she discovered me, fast asleep in the middle of the children's room.

"Good morning, hon."

I sat up immediately, blinking hard. I tried to read the librarian's expression. She didn't look angry, thank goodness, but she certainly did not look pleased.

"Good morning," I said. "I . . . I think I fell asleep."

"I think you did, too. Your parents are probably very, very worried right now, Charlotte. Do you want to use my phone to call them?"

She pulled a small, rectangular silver device out of her skirt pocket and tried to hand it to me. I stared at it.

"Do you know your parents' number?" the librarian asked.

"I'll just walk home," I told Miss Timms, standing up. "I don't need to ring them first. Thank you, though."

She shook her head. "I don't feel comfortable letting you do that. I need to know that you'll get home safely." When I didn't say anything, she looked deeply into my eyes, and I felt like she could see the truth in there. It was so obvious, how could she not? "Where are your parents?" she asked.

I didn't know what else to do, so I told the truth. "Dead."

"I'm so sorry," she said.

I shrugged.

"Who is your guardian, then? Do you live with other relatives, or friends, or . . . ?"

I pictured my relatives and friends: Justine, Thomas, Aunt Matilda, Kitty, Kitty, Kitty. "I suppose I don't live anywhere," I said.

I wondered whether Miss Timms would call the police. After all, I was a homeless girl hiding out in the children's room. Maybe I would wind up in an orphanage.

I thought again about Sara Crewe from *A Little Princess*. When she was orphaned, she got to stay at her posh London boarding school; she just had to sleep in the attic and work as an unpaid scullery maid. Maybe this librarian would send me to be a maid somewhere. I didn't know how to cook or clean really, but at least it would be a place to sleep.

But Miss Timms didn't call the police on me. Instead she said, "Come on, hon. Let me take you out for breakfast."

*   *   *

We walked to a restaurant down the street with a big shiny sign outside that said TONY'S DINER — 24 HRS. The waiter sat us at a booth with slippery seats and brought over menus that were twelve pages long. Really! There was a whole page just for eggs and a whole page just for sandwiches and another page still for beverages. I didn't recognize half the names of the foods, but that was all right because some of them had pictures, too.

"Order whatever you want," Miss Timms told me.

"None of this is rationed?" I asked.

"What do you mean?"

The last time I'd bought food, everything had been rationed: meat, sugar, eggs. Everything. Dad (or, more often lately, Justine and I) had to go to the shops with our ration books in order to get most foods, and then we were only allowed a little bit of everything. It was hard every week, when we reached the end of our rations and realized we were all out of butter or tea. Everybody got snippy with one another, even though it was Hitler's fault, not any of ours.

I hadn't realized how hungry I was. When the waiter came back to take our order, I pointed to everything I wanted: something called a grilled cheese sandwich, pork sausages, a chocolate milkshake. "And have you really got bananas?" I demanded.

"Yeah," the waiter said. "We really do."

"One of those, please. Actually, two, if that's all right."

The last time I'd had a banana was for Kitty's tenth birthday. She'd saved it especially for me. I don't know how or where she got it. I held on to it for days, drawing out the excitement.

By the time I finally could not stand to wait a minute longer, the banana had already gone brown and mushy. I ate it anyway. But it wasn't very good. "I love the way you say banana," Miss Timms commented after the waiter left. "Bah-nah-nah."

I smiled. "You say it funny."

She shrugged. "You say tom*ay*to, I say tom*ah*to." She took a sip of her water. "So, I guess now I understand why you've been spending so much time in the library, hmm? Where did you come from, Charlotte?"

That was one question I could answer truthfully. "Bristol."

Miss Timms tapped a fingernail against her water glass. "I don't know where that is."

"Southwest England," I said helpfully. "About one hundred and twenty miles west of London."

"Got it. So how did you get from the southwest of England to middle-of-nowhere Wisconsin, without any parents or guardians, carrying no belongings, and wearing nothing but a flannel pantsuit?"

"It's *pajamas*," I said.

She raised an eyebrow and waited.

I tried to think of what Kitty would say if she were here with me. Would she be able to find us a home, a way to start a new life? We had spent so much time talking about time travel, imagining all the different places we could explore. Now I realized that we had never discussed the details of how we would actually live when we got to a new place and time, having no money and knowing no one. And maybe that's why I'd been happy to talk about it—because I'd assumed it would never really happen.

If Kitty were here with me, everything would be different. Wherever this librarian sent us, at least she would send us there together. And I wouldn't be carrying around this heavy weight in my stomach, because if Kitty were here, I would not be the girl who jumped time and left her friend behind.

How stupid we had been. With our innocent, wide-eyed confidence. *Oh, of* course! *I'll just go to a tower that's four thousand miles and seventy-three years away from here, and there Kitty will be, waiting for me!*

What a rotten plan Kitty and I had come up with. And we'd thought ourselves so brilliant. As if we were any match for war, or happenstance, or time.

"Charlotte?" Miss Timms prompted.

I gave up. Miss Timms seemed so nice, and I was sick of lying and planning and hiding. I took a deep breath and said, "Do you believe in time travel?"

CHAPTER 11

The waiter brought over our meals: a mug of coffee and a dish of yogurt for Miss Timms, and two full plates heaped high with food, bananas on the side, and a milkshake for me.

"No," Miss Timms said with a smile. "I don't believe in time travel. Charlotte, you can tell me how you really ended up here. I won't get mad, no matter what it is. I promise."

My shoulders sank. But of course Miss Timms wouldn't believe me. In a world where no one had ever discovered the secrets of time travel, what had happened to me was wholly unbelievable.

I peeled open my first banana and took a bite. "Oh!" I cried. "It's even better than I remembered!"

Miss Timms smiled at me again, but her eyes were sad. "Are you okay, Charlotte?" she asked. "Has anyone hurt you? I hate to ask this, but . . . were you kidnapped? You can tell me anything, hon. I know you don't know me, but I promise, I'm on your side."

I could tell she was on my side, but there was nothing I could tell her. Yes, I had been kidnapped, but that was just about the least of my problems.

"Nobody hurt me," I said. "I'm fine. I'm just . . . lost, I think."

"Here's what we're going to do," Miss Timms said. She took a sip of coffee. "I have a friend who works for Child Services. We're going to go over to his office, and we'll see what he thinks. He'll probably interview you, and then put you in a foster home, at least for a little while, until they figure out who you really belong to. How does that sound?"

I liked that Miss Timms said "we," and I liked that she was really asking for my opinion, as though, should I say this was a bad idea, we wouldn't have to go through with it.

"Aren't you needed back at the library?" I asked.

She checked her watch, then sighed. "I wish. They've cut funding again, so now I'm officially only there from noon to six. I went early today to reshelve some books before we opened to the public. So, I definitely appreciate your concern, but I can get you to Child Services and back before anyone even starts to look for me. What do you say?"

"Fine," I said. "That sounds fine."

"Great!" Miss Timms said. "But first," she added, "let's finish eating."

*　*　*

Miss Timms's friend was a slender man with dark brown skin and very short hair. He introduced himself as "Christophe Babcock, but you can call me Chris," and I wondered why it was that both the American adults I'd met wanted to be called by their first names.

As Miss Timms had predicted, Mr. Babcock asked me a series of questions. He was very nice about all of them. There just wasn't anything I could tell him.

My name is Charlotte Bromley. I'm ten years old. I'm from Bristol, England. My father is Robert Bromley, and my mother is Elizabeth Bromley, and they are both dead. No known living relations. How did I get here? I don't know. Did anyone hurt me? No one to speak of. Will anyone come looking for me? Not likely.

"Jennifer tells me you think you might have time traveled here," Mr. Babcock said gently.

I shrugged noncommittally.

"You know," he said, "sometimes we like to believe that something happened to us, because that's easier than confronting whatever it is that actually *did* happen to us. Do you know what I mean?"

"Sort of," I said.

Mr. Babcock didn't seem that bothered by any of this, as if ten-year-old orphan girls often landed in his office with no explanation. Come to think of it, maybe they did. Maybe that's what working in Child Services meant. "Don't worry, Charlotte," he reassured me. "I'll work on finding any relatives you might have out there, anyone who could be wondering where you are. That's part of my job."

I gave him a weak smile. *Good luck with that, Mr. Babcock.*

Eventually Miss Timms had to go to work. "Please call me, or stop by the library, once you're settled," she asked. "I want to know that you're okay."

"Thank you for breakfast," I replied, and I watched her walk away from me.

I spent a long time waiting in Mr. Babcock's office. I didn't mind too much, though, since he had a shelf full of books. One of them was called *The Baby-Sitters Club #4: Mary Anne Saves the Day*, and I read almost all of it before Mr. Babcock said to me, "Charlotte, I've found a family for you to stay with. Do you want to go over to their house to meet them?"

"Yes . . ." I said dubiously, holding my place in the book with my finger.

"I promise they're very nice," he said. "You don't need to worry. I know it's been hard up to now, but you'll be safe there."

"I'm not worried," I told him. "I just . . . Could I stay here a little while longer? So I can finish the book?" I held up *The Baby-Sitters Club #4: Mary Anne Saves the Day*.

"You know what?" he said. "You can take it with you."

"Really?" I squealed. "Thank you ever so much, Mr. Babcock!"

He blinked a few times. "Just Chris is fine."

He drove me over to my new house. I liked it instantly. It was brick, considerably smaller than Jake and Noah's house, although it still had its own front yard. There were houses on either side, which made me feel better—the buildings on Jake's street were spaced so far from one another that it felt like an alien planet. Best of all, we drove past the library on the way, and the house seemed to be close by. I would be able to walk to visit Miss Timms.

A woman and man opened the door to the house as we stopped in front of it. They looked at least a decade older than my parents, maybe more. The woman was wearing trousers, an untucked button-down shirt, and silly pink sandals with big flowers on the toes. The man wore shorts with images of red fish sewn onto them.

"Hi, Chris!" the woman called as Mr. Babcock and I walked up the front stairs. She gave me a small hug and a kiss on the cheek. I tried not to flinch. "You must be Charlotte," she said, holding me back so she could look me in the eye. "Hi, Charlotte. Welcome home."

CHAPTER 12

The woman introduced herself as Melanie, and the man in the fish-patterned shorts said he was Keith. They didn't offer their surnames, so I reckoned "Melanie" and "Keith" were just what I had to call them. I tried to anagram their names but stopped as soon as I rearranged the letters in "Melanie" to spell "Mean lie."

Melanie—who did *not* seem like a mean liar—led us into the kitchen, and she and Keith spoke with Mr. Babcock for a while until eventually it was time for him to go.

"Call me if you need anything, Charlotte," Mr. Babcock said. "Anything at all. Here's my number and e-mail."

He handed me a little cream-colored card. I stared at it and didn't say anything.

"I'll be back to check on you tomorrow," Mr. Babcock went on. "But remember that you can call me twenty-four seven."

The numbers "twenty-four seven" were not printed on the cream-colored card, so I didn't know what Mr. Babcock meant. I also didn't know how I would call him, even if something terrible happened and I needed help right away. I hadn't yet seen a telephone anywhere in Melanie and Keith's house. Maybe they shared one with their neighbors.

After Mr. Babcock left, Melanie said, "Let me show you to your room, Charlotte."

I followed her up the stairs, looking at the framed photographs hanging all along the wall. There were loads of pictures of Melanie and Keith with a big dog and a girl who changed ages from photo to photo. Here they were on a boat, and the girl looked like she was my age, all freckles and tangled hair. Here they were in front of a fancy modern castle, and the girl couldn't have been older than four. Here they were again, and this time the girl was tall and even older than Justine, wearing a long black gown, like my dad when he went to Friday-night dinners at the university.

"That's our daughter, Penelope," Melanie explained, following my gaze. "And that big bozo of a dog was Snookums, who unfortunately died a few years ago. He's buried in the backyard. You can go take a look, if you like dog graves."

"I don't know if I like dog graves or not," I told her honestly.

Melanie opened a door at the top of the stairs. "This," she said, "is your bedroom."

I stepped inside. The walls were painted pink, and there was a bed in the corner with a matching pink-and-white eiderdown and loads of pink-and-white lace pillows. A small white desk sat in the corner, a little lamp perched on it.

The room was nice. And clean. And *untouched*.

A desperate longing surged up inside of me, and I rested my hand on the doorknob to steady myself. Out of all the things about my old life to miss, was I honestly missing my *bedroom*? That messy room I shared with Justine that constantly had our clothes strewn about the floor, the beds unmade, the corners unswept? I was an orphan now, but my room in 1940 looked far more like an orphanage than this new room did. Who would miss that?

But it kept overwhelming me. The continual remembering that I could never go back.

"I hope you like pink," Melanie said.

I used to like pink, because pink was Kitty's favorite color, which meant that it was my second-favorite color, just out of loyalty. But now I would sleep every night smothered by pink pillows that reminded me only of the way I left her.

"I don't know if I like pink or not."

Melanie sat down on the pink bed. I continued to stand. "I know you just got here," she said. "But do you have any questions for me? I'm happy to answer anything."

"Yes," I said, but then I couldn't work out what to ask. I had *so many* questions, but where to start? And which could I say without giving away that I was a time traveler?

Of course, I was starting to realize, if these people didn't believe in time travel, then nothing would give me away. They would never suspect the truth.

"Why?" I asked at last. Melanie didn't say anything, and I realized this wasn't enough of a question yet. "Why are you letting me stay with you?" I went on. "You don't even know me."

She nodded. "Keith and I have been taking in foster children for years. Ever since Penelope first left for college, and she's twenty-six now. She went to school out in Hawaii . . ." I must have looked blank, because Melanie elaborated. "It's *very* far away. So while the neighbors' kids were coming home from college every time they needed to do their laundry, Penelope came home for Christmas and that was it."

I was relieved to hear that they still had Christmas in the future, because that was our favorite holiday. Kitty would come over first thing on Christmas morning. Mum even prepared a stocking for her. We would eat a big breakfast with my family, and together we would pull our Christmas crackers and wear the paper crowns from them for the whole rest of the day. Then we would run over to the McLaughlins' house for a big turkey dinner, and we would open our second stockings of the day there. We would listen to the King's speech and go caroling. Kitty and I would walk across the Downs and along Whiteladies Road. Absolutely every shop was closed on Christmas, so no one else would be there, and with the street all to ourselves, we pretended that we were the owners and rulers of the whole city.

Without Kitty, maybe Christmas wasn't my favorite holiday anymore.

Melanie was still speaking. "We had this empty bedroom sitting here," she said, "so we figured, why not give a kid a home? You know, there are some people who just feel like being a parent is their true calling in life. That's how Keith and I are. Of course we have jobs—he works in minor league baseball, and I'm an event planner. But our *passion* is raising children. Penelope's long done being raised, as she'll be the first to tell you, but we weren't done with our roles yet."

This was all so foreign to me, and I don't just mean "American." I was pretty certain my parents had never felt that raising me, Justine, and Thomas was their "true calling in life." My dad's true calling was to unravel the mystery of time travel. And my mum's was . . . well, she had never said. But obviously it wasn't me.

"You're our fourth foster child," Melanie went on. "The other three were very happy here, and I hope you will be, too. I know it's a difficult transition, but with time I think you might realize that living here may be easier than . . . well, than whatever you left behind."

She said this carefully, as if I might tell her what I had left behind.

As if I could.

"Where did the other three go?" I asked.

"Back to their families." Melanie adjusted the pillows behind her, even though they already looked outrageously neat to me. "Sometimes parents go to jail for a while, or go missing for a while, or go somewhere to deal with their problems for a while. That's where foster families step in. But when the parents are ready to be parents again, they get their kids back. We're always sad to give the kids up, because we love them, but their parents love them, too, and that's the deal."

I wondered how Melanie would feel if she knew that my parents were definitely never ever going to be ready to be parents again. She would never have to be sad to give *me* up.

"Do you have anything you want to unpack?" Melanie asked.

I held my hands out to the sides so she could see they were empty.

"Not to worry. I have most everything Penelope ever wore. I'm sure we can find something that will fit you. Let me go look in the attic."

Melanie left the room, and I stood in the middle of it, alone, and tried to think of a plan.

Then I realized that I couldn't think of a plan because there *was* no plan. This was it. This was my life. My life was soundless cars and grilled cheese sandwiches and pink walls and inexplicably chilly buildings in inexplicably hot weather, and there was no choice about any of that.

The thought filled me with terror. This could not be it. I could not live like this forever. I would go mad. I pressed my face to the closed window, like an animal in a cage.

I turned back around when Melanie returned carrying a cardboard box labeled PENELOPE, 10 YRS. "Clearly all these clothes are from sixteen years ago, so I apologize that you're not going to be the height of modern fashion in them." She set the box down on the desk. "But this will do until we can go shopping. I'm sure we can find something in here that's a little more summery than what you've got on."

I nodded. My pajamas had long ago started to feel grimy.

Melanie left me alone to change. I opened the box and started taking out clothes. Sixteen years ago would be 1997. Apparently girls in 1997 wore a lot of brightly colored shirts with pictures of footballs on them and phrases like "Sutton Town Soccer."

I took off my pajamas and folded them up at the end of Penelope's bed. I would never have bothered to do that in my own room, but here everything looked so neat that I felt like I should be neat, too.

I changed into a purple corduroy skirt and one of the football shirts, and then I stood in front of the mirror. In Penelope's old clothes, I didn't look like myself anymore. But I didn't look like Penelope, either, or at least not the Penelope I had seen in that photograph of her and her family on a boat. Penelope was redheaded and muscular and tanned, and I was none of that.

I looked like a stranger. Like an imaginary girl from the future.

I touched my hand to the mirror, and I made a promise to my reflection: "I will find a way out of this," I whispered. "I will find a way home."

Chapter 13

Melanie woke me early the next morning, flinging open Penelope's pink curtains. It was another sunny day. Three in a row. If this had happened in Bristol, Mum would be mumbling darkly about how this much pleasant weather foretold "a long winter," or some rubbish like that. Mum had always been suspicious of too much sun. And ever since the Battle of Britain had started, I'd seen her point: Clear skies made it much easier for German bombs to find their targets.

"Up and at 'em, Charlotte," Melanie said, pulling back Penelope's pink-and-white eiderdown. "We need to get you some new clothes before school starts. You don't want to wear one of Penelope's old soccer tees on your first day. What will the other girls think?"

My stomach tightened, and I wanted to pull the blankets right back over my head. It hadn't occurred to me until this very moment that I would have to go to a new school, with new girls, and no Kitty by my side.

Maybe schools in the future were different. Maybe all the students here were really friendly to everybody, even to bookish girls in glasses. Humans had invented the Internet and artificial cooling systems; surely they could have invented a way for kids to be nice.

But I wasn't holding my breath.

I was going to find a way home. I was. I had to. But I hadn't the foggiest notion how, or when, and I had to admit that the school term would probably start before I, a lone ten-year-old girl, had worked out the secret to time travel.

Within an hour, Melanie and I were at an enormous place that she called "the mall." It was the biggest building I had ever seen. It was far bigger than Wills Tower, bigger even than the Houses of Parliament, which had stunned me with their grandness when we went on holiday to London.

Melanie decided we should start at a colorful, glittery store that sold only clothes for girls. "I'm thinking we should get you a few pairs of jeans," she said, flipping through the racks with expert speed. "And a pair or two of shorts, I guess, even though summer's almost over. And leggings. And obviously T-shirts, some long-sleeved tees, sneakers . . . I love to shop, don't you?"

She waited for my reply. I wasn't sure what to say. At last I settled on, "What are sneakers?"

Melanie blinked a few times. "Isn't it funny?" she said after a moment. "You'd think America and England would basically be the same, since we speak the same language. But they aren't actually the same at all, are they?"

I shook my head. "I don't know."

"Here." Melanie handed me a pile of clothes. "These"— she pointed to the pink plimsolls on top—"are sneakers. Why don't you try everything on, and we can figure out what your personal style is?"

The tone of Melanie's voice made me suspect that figuring out your personal style was a tremendously exciting and important thing to do.

"I didn't used to get a personal style," I told her. "My mum made all our clothes."

Melanie raised her eyebrows. "Your mum," she said, "must be superhuman."

Melanie sent me into a fitting room. Nobody seemed to work in this colorful, glittery store. It wasn't like the few times I'd gone to Selfridges in London with Mum, where there'd been shopgirls who measured you and waited on you. Here they just closed you in a small room with a mirror and left you alone.

I tried on a pair of very tight trousers and a sleeveless top with the word LOLLIPOP written on it in rainbow-colored letters. I looked at myself in the mirror and giggled. I imagined what Kitty would say, if she were here. "'Lollipop'? Like in *The Wizard of Oz*? My goodness, Americans do wear the most peculiar things, don't they?"

My smile faded. I shouldn't be giggling. Girls who let their best friends die ought not giggle ever again.

"Come on out here, Charlotte!" Melanie called. "Let's see."

I opened the door and stepped out of the dressing room. "You look so cute!" Melanie exclaimed. "We *have* to get that tank top."

Melanie was not alone. Next to her stood another woman and a girl who looked to be about my age. They both had straight, shiny, chestnut-brown hair, like horses' manes. My hair immediately felt even messier and frizzier than usual.

"This is Luanne Fulton," Melanie introduced the woman. "And her daughter, Dakota."

"Dakota" did not sound like a name to me. It sounded like a place to store winter clothing.

"We're here doing some back-to-school shopping for Dakota, too, and we just ran into Melanie," Mrs. Fulton explained.

I tittered, and everyone looked at me. "Sorry," I mumbled, not wanting to explain that I'd stopped listening while anagramming Dakota Fulton's name to "a fat loud knot."

"It's *so* nice to meet you, Charlotte," Mrs. Fulton said to me in a childlike voice. "You're such a brave kid."

I stopped smiling. I didn't feel brave. Yes, I was at the mall, shopping for clothes when every single person I knew and loved was gone. But that wasn't *brave*. It was just keeping calm and carrying on—because what other choice did I have?

"After all you've been through . . ." Mrs. Fulton raised her eyebrows, as if waiting for me to fill in with a description of what I'd been through.

"Mmm," I murmured.

Mrs. Fulton's eyebrows went back to normal.

"So have you decided what color to paint the house?" Melanie asked Mrs. Fulton, distracting her. The two of them started talking, some grown-up conversation that did not include me.

"You're going into fifth grade, too?" Dakota said to me, ignoring them.

I had no idea. I glanced to Melanie for help.

"Oh, I bet they call it something different in England," Dakota said. "How old are you?"

"Ten."

"When's your birthday?"

"The eighteenth of October."

Dakota's forehead crinkled. "You're turning eleven on October eighteenth? That's less than two months from now. So you should actually be going into *sixth* grade."

Drat. The maths of time travel kept tripping me up. When I left in 1940, it had been October, and I had only just turned ten. Now it was August 2013—nearly time for my birthday again!

Maybe I should say yes and collect another round of birthday presents from my new parents. Maybe I should find a way to keep time traveling to summers past and future, so it would always be nearly my birthday, and I could continually get new books and sweets.

But I didn't really think I could pass for eleven. Especially not here in America, where so many of the children I'd seen in the mall so far seemed *bigger*, somehow. Not fatter, necessarily, but sturdier. Like girls whose food had never been rationed, whose sky never ran out of sun.

So I said, "Sorry! That's an English thing. I got confused. My tenth birthday was actually in July."

"Mine, too!" Dakota squealed. "What day?"

"Eighteenth," I said. Then my stomach twisted suddenly, and I had to steady myself against the wall. The eighteenth of July wasn't my birthday. It was Kitty's.

"Mine is the ninth," Dakota said. "I'm nine days older than you."

She seemed to be expecting some sort of reward for this accomplishment, so I said, "Well done, you."

"So," she went on, dropping her voice a little. "You're an *orphan*?"

"I suppose so," I replied.

"Oh my *gosh*!" Dakota clapped her hand to her mouth. "That's so cool."

"Is it?"

"*Yes.* I wish I was an orphan, like, every day. You get to do whatever you want . . . no parents, no stupid rules or bedtimes or limits on how much TV you can watch. . . . Plus it's so *romantic.*"

Maybe I had once agreed with that, when I read *A Little Princess* and dreamt of living in an attic. But now I knew better. I considered telling Dakota about my two nights in the library, stealing goldfish crackers and scavenging sandwiches out of rubbish bins, sleeping on chairs and hiding in bookcases. Was that *romantic*?

"And you're British," Dakota told me, as if I might not know.

"I'm *English*," I corrected her.

"What's the difference?"

I blinked at her. It seemed so obvious that I'd never actually thought about how to explain it. "Well, I was born in England. And my parents and their parents and *their* parents were born in England. If you said I was *British*, you might mean I was from Wales or Scotland—"

"Is that worse?" Dakota interrupted. "To be from Wales or Scotland or wherever?"

"Of course not," I said, even though I sort of believed that it was.

"Either way," she said, "it's supercute."

"Being English?"

"Yeah. It's pretty much the cutest. Oh my *gosh*, I just want to eat you up!" She grabbed and squeezed my shoulders.

"D," Mrs. Fulton said, coming back into our conversation, "you own that lollipop tank, don't you?" She pointed at my sleeveless top.

"Yup."

"Then you girls better make sure you don't accidentally wear it on the same day!" She laughed.

"No, Mom, that's actually an *awesome* idea!" Dakota said. "Charlotte, let's both wear our lollipop shirts on the first day of school. I'll get Sydney and Kianna to do it, too. That way everyone will know we're together. Perfect, right?"

Mrs. Fulton rolled her eyes. "Kids!" she said to Melanie. Then, to her daughter, "Come on, D, we have a lot more shopping to do before we can leave. Say bye to Charlotte."

"Bye!" Dakota took a few steps away with her mother, then whirled back around to face me, her shiny hair whipping across her shoulders. She pointed at me. "And you *have* to sit with us at recess on the first day. Okay? 'Cause I found you first!" She threw a big smile at Melanie and me, then left for good.

"Well," Melanie said with a laugh, "at least we know we're definitely getting this shirt! If Luanne's kid likes it, I'm sure it's the height of fashion."

I didn't say anything. I just went back into the dressing room with my piles of strange clothes.

Dakota wanted to sit with me at school. She wanted to be friends with me. I had a friend in the future now. And that was exactly what I needed.

So why did I still feel like I was going to be sick?

CHAPTER 14

When the first day of school came, ten days later, I was ready for it.

Well, not exactly. But I *was* ready to get out of Melanie and Keith's house.

They were perfectly nice. But they were always *there*. Both of them worked from the house so much of the time, and if one of them had a meeting somewhere else, they made sure the other was staying at home with me. Even if I was just going out to their backyard to play, Melanie would move her laptop computer and telephone to the deck, so she could watch me. I didn't so much feel like pretending to be a woodland fairy, or a lost princess, when my real-life foster parents were sitting a few feet away. And I *certainly* couldn't start trying to find a way to time travel home when every few minutes someone was asking me if I wanted a glass of lemonade or if I'd hurt myself badly when I stubbed my toe on the porch step.

For the first time, I really understood how Kitty must have felt, having parents who never left her alone. Kind of, well, trapped. Trapped in their world.

And what good had it done the McLaughlins? For all that they watched Kitty, they weren't able to save her.

I read a lot, of course. Just as much as I had in Bristol, and then some, filling my mind with made-up lives so I wouldn't have to think about my own. But what was oddest about Melanie and Keith was this: They didn't read books. At all.

It wasn't because they were constantly working, like my dad. They had free time, but they spent it going to the gym, or doing things on their computers, or watching the television. They just *did not read*. They had bookcases, but they were filled only with knickknacks and framed photographs. One day, out of sheer boredom, I went up to the attic and looked through all of Penelope's old boxes, expecting at least one of them to hold books. But they were all filled just with clothing, jewelry, and silvery round objects that Melanie told me were called "CDs."

"Penelope was never really a reader," Melanie said, like this explained things.

I finished *The Baby-Sitters Club #4: Mary Anne Saves the Day* on my second day at Melanie and Keith's house, and by my fifth day there I had read the only other books I could find: one called *The World Is Flat*, which explained many things about the twenty-first century—but also raised more questions for me than it answered—and one called *The Da Vinci Code*, which was confusing but dramatic and involved a lot of running around Paris for some reason.

"I never actually read it," Keith said, when he saw me flying through *The Da Vinci Code*. "I heard good things, though."

When I looked around the house and saw no books left, I went back to the library. And I kept going, every single day. At first Melanie or Keith insisted on driving me there and back, but when they realized how much time I wanted to spend there, they gave up.

I loved being at the library. Miss Timms showed me more and more ways to use the Internet, and I continued to read my way alphabetically through the books in the children's room. My only rule for myself was that I not read anything I had read in Bristol. Those books made me too sad. So no *Little Princess*. No *Wizard of Oz*. I was a new girl with a new name, a new country, and a new birthday. I didn't need any books to remind me of the life I'd lost.

I also spent some of my library time researching time travel, trying to find a way home. I knew my dad had said that if you went through a portal, you had to accept that you could *never* go back. And my dad always knew what he was talking about.

But what if there was another way? Instead of just waiting for another portal to open up in front of me, which I understood was impossible, what if I could make my *own* way back? Build a time travel machine, or find a genie who would grant me three wishes, or . . . something?

If there was any hope of that, I had to try. I would go back to the day we were taken, the day of Kitty's Film Stars invitation, and I would tell her to leave me, to go to the cinema with Betsy and Margaret and Jeanine. Or I would go back even further than that, to before my mum went away, and I would find a way to make her stay.

But nothing at the library seemed helpful. Articles that promised "easy ways to time travel!" were rubbish, filled with theoretical musings that only my dad would have been able to parse, or advice to "let go of fear and set your mind free."

I tried that, by the way. I would try anything, no matter how silly it sounded. I let go of fear, but I didn't time travel anywhere. I just nodded off for a few minutes.

I read one book where the kids held a séance to conjure up the dead, and that seemed like a good idea—maybe I could call up the ghost of my dad and ask him how I could get home again. Or I could call up Kitty, and even if I couldn't go anywhere, at least I could tell her that I was sorry.

But I couldn't have a séance alone. I needed friends for that. And I didn't reckon that Miss Timms and Mr. Babcock would be terribly helpful. So I just kept reading, and thinking, and imagining.

By the end of summer, I was in the library from the minute it opened until the minute it closed. Unfortunately, that was only noon to six p.m., Tuesday through Saturday. All the rest of my time, I was just home. At Melanie and Keith's house. Watching them watching me.

So I could not *wait* for school to start.

Melanie drove me to Sutton Brook Elementary on my first day. I wore my lollipop top, just as Dakota had ordered. Even though I knew I shouldn't, I spent the car ride picking at the glitter on the shirt, peeling off small bits into my hand.

"Are you nervous?" Melanie asked as we pulled up in front of the school.

I gave her a dark look. *What do you think?*

Melanie laughed. "I'm sure you'll make many new friends," she said.

I wasn't sure of that at all. I was sure *Penelope*, as a child, had made many new friends. Penelope, who had boxes filled with her personal style, who played a sport, who was "never really a reader." But for all that I slept in Penelope's bed and sat in Penelope's seat at the dinner table, I was not her. I was *Charlotte*, whoever that might turn out to be.

Melanie gave me a hug good-bye. I got out of the car and walked slowly into the playground, which was already filled with children running around, playing on the swings, shrieking. I was supposed to stay out here until the fifth-grade teacher, Mrs. Vasquez, called us to line up.

I looked around for a place where I could sit down and read my book. I was just about to settle on an unclaimed sliver of grass when I heard a voice call, "Charlotte! Hey!"

I turned around.

"Jake!" I exclaimed, thrilled to see a familiar face. "Hullo! All right, are you?"

He looked down at himself, his face perplexed, as if expecting to see a stain on the front of his shirt. "Why wouldn't I be all right?" he asked.

"Oh—I just meant—how are you doing? How was the rest of your summer?"

"Oh, I get it." Jake's face turned red. "Yeah, I'm good. We were at Lake Michigan for the past week for a big family reunion thing."

"Smashing!" I exclaimed.

"Yeah!" Jake's blush faded now. "It was awesome. On the last night we built this big bonfire, and I ate *six* s'mores. *And* I beat my older cousin at Chubby Bunnies, even though he's fifteen and his cheeks are huge." Jake stuck his fingers in the corners of his mouth and pulled them apart, to demonstrate. "I almost threw up," he added.

I giggled. "I don't know what s'mores are, though," I said. "Or Chubby Bunnies."

"Really?" Jake's eyebrows widened. "You don't make s'mores in England?"

"I don't know."

"Charlotte," Jake said, very seriously. "S'mores are the best food in the world. You should come over sometime and we can make them on the grill." He paused, then added hastily, "I mean, only if you want to."

"Of course I want to, silly," I said.

He smiled widely, showing off crooked teeth and too much gum. "Hey, whose class are you in?"

"Mrs. Vasquez's," I replied.

"Me, too!" Jake jumped up and down twice, then stopped abruptly. "I mean, that's cool that we're in the same class. Yeah. Noah had Mrs. Vasquez for fifth grade, too, and he liked her. Well, he's Noah, so he's never actually *liked* a teacher. But he said she let them play Seven-Up sometimes at the end of the day, and she never assigned weekend homework, so that's good, I guess."

"Probably," I agreed.

"Hey," Jake went on. "When you come over, we can also play . . ."

He faded to silence, staring at something behind me. I turned around.

It was Dakota.

"Hullo!" I said, pleased to see another familiar face. Maybe starting school would be better than I'd thought.

As promised, Dakota was wearing the same lollipop shirt, though I could tell that she hadn't picked any of the glitter off hers. She wrinkled her nose at Jake, then said to me, as if he wasn't even there, "Hi, Charlotte! Oh my gosh, you look *adorable*. Come on, let me introduce you to Sydney and Kianna. They're totally dying to meet you."

She grabbed my hand and pulled me away. "Good-bye, Jake!" I called behind me. He did not reply.

"Look," Dakota said in a low voice, slowing the pace once we were far enough away from Jake, "I get that you're new here, so you probably don't know this yet, but—don't hang out with Jake Adler."

"Why not?" I twisted my head around to look back at him. He was still standing in the spot where I'd left him, staring down at the grass.

"He's not cool," Dakota explained.

"How can you tell?"

"I don't have to tell," Dakota said. "I just know."

We stopped at a tree where two girls in matching lollipop shirts were already standing. "This is Sydney, and this is Kianna," Dakota introduced them.

"Hullo." I waved.

"Look at you!" Sydney shrieked. "You are exactly as cute as Dakota said you were."

"Say something!" Kianna demanded.

My eyes darted from Kianna to Dakota, hoping for some more guidance than that. At last I said, "Something?"

"Say something *British*," Kianna explained. "Like 'bangers and mash.'"

"Bangers and mash," I repeated, and the three girls squealed in unison.

"Why can't I hang out with Jake Adler?" I asked.

"*So* cute," Sydney commented.

"Ew," Dakota said.

Sydney blushed. "I meant her accent, not Jake Adler! He's gross."

"Why?" I asked again.

"He talks to himself sometimes," Dakota explained. "He keeps a collection of action figures in his desk, and he majorly freaked out last year when he couldn't find one. He plays on the swing set during recess. By himself. Like we're in kindergarten."

"And his favorite class is *art*," Kianna added. "He's always drawing little pictures or doing watercolors or gluing colored paper on to things. Like he's a *girl*."

"And I don't think he ever learned to tie his shoes," Sydney contributed.

"And his mom leaves him notes in his *Star Wars* lunchbox," Dakota said, and the three girls howled with laughter. "I took one off his desk once when he wasn't looking," Dakota added. "It said, 'May the Force be with you today, Jake! Love, Mommy.'" They collapsed into giggles again.

I stared at these girls, these girls who wore the same shirt as me but seemed so different. I tried to laugh with them, but I couldn't understand. What were action figures? What was a *Star Wars* lunchbox? Why were any of these things bad?

All I knew about Jake was that he had helped me when I arrived in Sutton, alone and lost. That seemed good, to me.

But what did I know about what was good in America in the year 2013? What did I know about "coolness"?

Only what Dakota and her friends told me. Nothing more.

"Fifth grade!" a short older woman shouted from the steps of the school.

"That's Mrs. Vasquez!" Dakota held on to one of my hands and Sydney took the other. Together, my new friends and I queued up with the rest of our classmates.

I looked around for Jake, wondering whether I would be able to tell, when I looked at him, that he was not cool. Would it be obvious to me, now that I knew what I was looking for?

But when I found him, standing alone at the back of the queue, he didn't seem not-cool. He just seemed sad. And he didn't meet my eyes.

"Fifth graders, let's go!" Mrs. Vasquez called.

I turned back around to face the front, and I followed the teacher into school.

Chapter 15

The morning of my first day of school wasn't as bad as I'd feared. Maths is the same anywhere. In Social Studies we were doing American history, which I knew nothing about, but from what I could tell, *nobody* knew anything about American history yet. Mrs. Vasquez said we would learn. In English we were each given a shiny new paperback of a book called *The Giver*. I hadn't got to that one at the library yet, since I was still on the *A*s, and this author's last name was Lowry.

Then it was time for lunch and break. As soon as I got out to the playground, Dakota grabbed me and dragged me to the top of the brightly colored metal climbing structure with her. Sydney and Kianna were already up there.

"Charlotte," Dakota said, her voice unusually deep. "Welcome to the Top of the Playground."

I giggled. She sounded ridiculous.

Kianna and Sydney did not giggle. Dakota narrowed her eyes and shook out her horse-mane hair. "I'm serious," she said. "Maybe you don't already know this because you're new here, but getting to hang out up here is a *very* big deal."

"Probably the biggest," Sydney contributed.

"Last year's fifth graders promised this spot to the three of us," Dakota went on. "And we are sharing it with you. No one else can come up here except for people who we say are worthy."

"Oh." When she put it like that, it did sound like a big deal. "Thank you," I added. I looked down at the rest of the playground and imagined briefly that I lived in outer space, staring down on the inhabitants of the foreign planet Earth. "What do you play up here?" I asked, hoping Dakota would answer "Martians."

Dakota did not say "Martians." She said, "Truth or Dare."

"Oh," I said. Again. I was so tired of saying "Oh." *Why don't you come to my time?* I kept wanting to scream at everyone. *See how well you can fake understanding things!*

"You have to choose either Truth or Dare," Dakota explained. "If you choose Truth, you have to answer whatever question I choose *completely truthfully*. No lies, no matter how embarrassing. And if you choose Dare, you have to do whatever dare I assign you. So, for example, Kianna—Truth or Dare?"

"Truth," Kianna answered, swinging her legs back and forth between the metal bars.

Sydney and Dakota groaned. "You *always* choose Truth," Sydney complained. "You're such a wimp."

Kianna shrugged. "I like Truths."

"Fine," Dakota said. "Truth: Which of the boys in our class would you want to be your boyfriend?"

"Dylan Cooper," Kianna answered. While Dakota and Sydney shrieked, I looked down on the playground and tried to remember which of the cap-wearing boys was Dylan Cooper. Then I tried to decide which of the boys I would want to be *my* boyfriend, but I didn't know anything about any of them, and also I didn't want a boyfriend, so this seemed like a pointless exercise.

Truth or Dare, I thought. *Dear Hurt Rot. Rather Tudor. Hard Torture.*

Hard Torture seemed most accurate.

"So do you get how the game is played?" Dakota asked me.

"Yes," I said. "Do you want to play Martians instead?"

Kianna and Sydney sputtered with laughter.

"*No*," Dakota snapped. "We are playing Truth or Dare. Charlotte! Truth or Dare?"

I bit my lip. *Truth* may have been the easier choice for Kianna, but it seemed to be the much harder choice for me. *Truth, Charlotte: Why are you an orphan? Truth, Charlotte: How did you wind up in Sutton, Wisconsin?*

The truth would do me no favors. "Dare," I said.

"See, *Charlotte* isn't a wimp," Sydney murmured. Kianna elbowed her, and Sydney squealed dramatically. "Are you *trying* to push me off?"

"Will you two shut up and help me think of a Dare for Charlotte?" Dakota said.

Immediately the three of them leaned their heads in together and started whispering. I couldn't make out what they were saying. But how bad could a Dare be, anyway? From a girl who has already lost everything, what more could they take?

Dakota, Sydney, and Kianna separated their heads and leaned back to look at me.

"Dare," Dakota said. "I dare you to tell Jake Adler that he's a big fat baby."

The playground grew still and silent for a moment. The chatter of my classmates below me faded into nothing. Kianna and Sydney watched me the way Aunt Matilda's cat used to watch budgies in their cages: with wordless, captivated delight.

"Why?" I asked.

"Because," Dakota said, "he *is* a big fat baby."

"But why do I have to tell him that?"

"Because those are the rules."

I blinked a few times. "I'll get in trouble," I said. "He'll tell Mrs. Vasquez, and I'll get in trouble." I assumed that happened at schools everywhere, even in America, even in the future.

But the three girls were already shaking their heads. "Jake won't tell," Dakota assured me.

"How do you know?"

Dakota shrugged. "Because he never does."

Well, maybe he should, I thought. But then I thought about what I did when Betsy, Margaret, and Jeanine told me that I couldn't be a Film Star, because I acted too young, because I liked to read, because I wore glasses, *because I was me.*

I did nothing.

So I could believe that Jake would do nothing, too.

Dakota and her friends were the Film Stars of Sutton Brook Elementary School. It was obvious. They dressed different, they talked different—but underneath all that, they were the same. Cruel and self-important, because they could be.

I could have walked away. I could have said, "Oh, sod your blooming game," climbed all the way down from the Top of the Playground, and tried to make different friends.

What would happen, if I said no? These girls would hate me, I assumed. I would no longer be the clueless orphan with the cute accent and the romantic life story. They would most likely turn on me and treat me as they did Jake and try to make me miserable for however long I stayed in Sutton.

And maybe I would be able to make different friends, better friends—but maybe I wouldn't. There are only so many Kittys in the world, and I had already been lucky enough to have one of them in my life. I didn't expect to find another Kitty waiting for me here at Sutton Brook Elementary School.

Especially considering that I had abandoned the first one.

But none of that, really, was the reason I climbed down the metal structure and walked across the playground to Jake, with the other girls close at my heels. I could have lived with them hating me, I could have lived as a lonely outsider. I could have been brave enough to make that choice. But I didn't, and this is why:

Ever so occasionally, you come to a moment when everything about you is tested. When you must decide, with one action, what kind of friend and person you want to be. I knew this because I had already come to such a moment: when I was given the chance to stand by Kitty's side, or to let her die alone. And at that moment, I had already decided what kind of person I was: the bad kind. The kind who could not be trusted.

You cannot do something so drastic and expect not to have to pay for it. We get what we deserve.

I used to know who I was. As my obituary had said: I was Elizabeth and Robert's daughter; Justine and Thomas's sister. I was in Miss Dickens's class at the Westminster School for Girls; I lived at 30 Orchard Close; I'd been born on October 18, 1930. I was Lottie Bromley. And Lottie Bromley would not have followed Dakota's orders.

But now all of that was gone. All those things that defined my life had been sucked up by the past, leaving behind not even a photograph to prove that they'd once been mine.

Without any of that, who was I?

I was Charlotte now. I had to forget Lottie. I had to move forward. And that's why I took the Dare.

I crossed that playground and stopped in front of Jake. He was sitting alone, drawing something in the dirt with a stick, mumbling to himself.

Jake looked up at me and smiled, then stopped smiling when he saw Dakota, Sydney, and Kianna behind me.

"Hey," he said.

"Hullo," I said. There was a lump in my throat, so I could barely get out my next sentence, but I rasped it out as best I could. "Jake, you're a big fat baby."

It was obvious that I didn't mean it. My words sounded hollow, forced, and fake. But sometimes we do things that we don't mean, and they hurt every bit as much as if we meant them.

Jake's head drooped, but he didn't run to tell Mrs. Vasquez, and he didn't fight back. And my new friends shrieked with laughter. I was one of them now.

That was the first way that I paid penance for what I had done to Kitty. But it didn't make me feel better. Until I found my way back to her, I would be paying for Kitty for the rest of my life.

Chapter 16

"Melanie tells me your first day of school went well," Keith said to me over supper that night.

"I suppose so." I cast about for something positive to say. All I came up with was, "I'm hopeless at American history."

For some reason this made Melanie and Keith laugh. We were eating in front of the television, which, I'd come to realize from the two weeks I'd lived with them, was where they always ate dinner. They had a big dining room with a long table, but I had never seen them use it. We mostly ate takeaway food. Tonight we were having something called burritos. They were quite nice.

Before Mum left, she used to cook for us every night. She made a lovely Sunday roast, and she knew how to make a ration card stretch. But after she left, we more often than not ate plain jam on bread, or whatever Justine brought home from the fish and chip shop. So I didn't mind the takeaway at Melanie and Keith's. It was better than what I'd grown used to.

"What are you thinking about doing for extracurriculars?" Melanie asked.

I stared at her blankly. I thought about saying "Oh," as usual, but it didn't seem like it would fit here.

"She means after-school activities," Keith explained. "Like soccer."

Over the past two weeks, I had learned two things. One, "soccer" was what Americans in the future called "football." Two, Penelope had been an absolute soccer champ. What I did not learn, because I had already known it, was that I was rubbish at sport and would not be following in Penelope's footsteps any time soon.

"Must I have extracurriculars?" I asked.

"You don't *have* to," Keith began.

"But it's a good idea," Melanie finished. "Especially since you're new in town. Activities are a wonderful way to make friends. And it will make you well-rounded."

I didn't know what "well-rounded" meant, exactly, but I was fairly certain I did not want to be it.

"Plus," Keith added, "you don't really want to spend every afternoon hanging around with us old folks, do you?"

It occurred to me then that maybe *he* did not want to spend every afternoon hanging around with *me*.

"You could join the school band," Melanie suggested. "Do you play an instrument?"

I shook my head. "But my mum sings," I blurted out. I didn't know why. It was true, though, wasn't it? The obituary had said that it was true.

Melanie and Keith glanced at each other quickly. I had told them almost nothing about my parents, and I could tell that they had been trying hard not to ask too much, not to push me. I could almost see them filing this fact away with the few others that they had: *Charlotte is from England, she's ten years old, and her mother sings.*

"Dance classes?" Melanie offered next. "Ballet or something?"

"Chess team?" Keith said.

"Oh, honey, be serious. Do you think the girls are going to be friends with the new kid on the chess team?"

"Mostly I just like to read," I said. I thought about adding *and play pretend*, but I didn't. "Can't I read for my extracurricular?"

Melanie just shook her head, turned back to the television, and unmuted *Beach Bums*, her favorite program.

The question of extracurriculars was still bothering me after school the next day, when I stopped by the library to say hello to Miss Timms and get a new book.

Today Miss Timms was a million places at once: picking up magazines that had been left on the ground, showing a young woman how to look for a new job on the computer, and trying to help an old man find a book with print big enough that he could read it without his glasses. I followed her around like a little puppy.

"I'm sorry to be so busy today, hon," she said as she hurried down an aisle of books, straightening spines as she went. "Now that school is back in session and everyone is home from summer vacation, I'm finding it really hard to get everything done. There's just not enough time! Anyway, not your problem. How are you liking school?"

I shrugged. Today Dakota had got new pencils, and Kianna, Sydney, and I had to spend most of the day admiring them. They were imported, Dakota told us. From Japan.

"I feel you," Miss Timms agreed, even though I hadn't spoken. "Settling into a new school is never easy. My dad was in the military when I was growing up, so we moved four times before I was even your age! When I was a teenager, I went to boarding school just so I wouldn't have to deal with packing up my bags and trying to make new friends every two years. It's hard."

"Not only that," I said, "but Melanie and Keith told me I need to have extracurriculars. Like soccer. Or the chess team."

"Well," Miss Timms said thoughtfully as she restarted a computer that wasn't working properly, "that's not a bad idea. Activities are a good way to make friends with similar interests to yours."

I frowned. I'd expected that Miss Timms would be on my side. She often seemed like the one person who was. "But I never had to have extracurriculars at home. I don't see why I should start now."

"What did you do at home, then?" Miss Timms asked.

"I read books, of course." I sighed. "I reckon Melanie and Keith just want me out of the house so they don't have to watch me all the time. Not that they *do* have to watch me all the time, even if I was there. But I think they *feel* like they do. I wish I could just stay here with you all day."

Miss Timms paused. It was the first time I'd seen her stop moving since I got to the library that day. "That's a great idea, hon," she said. "Do you want to work here?"

"At the library?" I felt my eyes grow wide.

"Yes. You'd be a big help to me. You could take care of the shelving when I'm too busy to do it. I can even teach you how to check out books. That would free me up enormously to work on some of my bigger projects that I can't seem to ever find the time for. And fund-raising, obviously." She made a face. "I feel like half my job is fund-raising sometimes. The depressing half. Anyway, I couldn't pay you very much, I'm afraid, but I could give you a small stipend. What do you say?"

My mouth was hanging open a little. "You'd trust me with all that?"

"Charlotte," Miss Timms said, leaning in closer. "When it comes to books, I trust you one hundred percent."

"I would love to," I said. "I would love, love, *love* to work here!"

Miss Timms chuckled. "Excellent! Then all we need to do is get permission from your foster parents."

How odd, I thought, that these two near-strangers would be able to stop me from doing something that I wanted so badly, just because they were grown-ups and somebody had told them that they were in charge.

But Melanie and Keith didn't say no. They said if working at the library was what I wanted my extracurricular to be, they would give me their full support. (Then they added that if I ever decided I *did* want ballet lessons, after all, I should just tell them.) So I went to the library almost every day after school. I got better and better at using the Internet. I learned how to read the labels on books to figure out where every one belonged. Soon I could answer almost every question about where to find books on different subjects.

After I'd been in Sutton for nearly two months, going to school, working at the library, and quietly fitting in, I gathered the courage to ask my new friends if they would hold a séance with me, like the kids I'd read about in that book. "Wouldn't it be brilliant if we could conjure an actual *ghost*?" I said.

It was recess, and we were sitting back on the Top of the Playground, even though the autumn chill had started nipping at our skin. I'd worried that my friends would respond to the séance as dismissively as when I'd asked if we could play Martians. But instead they loved the idea—even Dakota, who I quickly had learned did not often love ideas unless they were her own.

"A séance! Can we do it right now?" Kianna asked.

"No," Dakota told her with authority. "We have to do it in the dark, and with a Ouija board or a crystal ball. We have to create an atmosphere that a ghost would be comfortable coming to."

I didn't know where Dakota had gotten her expertise on séances, but I was glad for it.

"We can do it at my house on Saturday," Sydney suggested. "We can have a slumber party! I'll ask my mom, but I'm sure she'll be okay with it."

"And we can order pizza!" Kianna suggested, bouncing up and down.

"And watch a scary movie," Dakota added.

"And have the séance," I reminded them. "The séance is the important part."

On Saturday evening, Keith dropped me off at Sydney's house. As Kianna had hoped, Sydney's mom ordered us a couple of pizzas, though we had to share them with

Sydney's little sisters, who kept begging me to say "British" things. I was glad the kids at school had already tired of that game. It was boring.

After dinner we watched a movie, though not a scary one, because Sydney's stepdad said that her sisters had to watch with us and it couldn't be anything that would give them nightmares. Dakota whispered to me, "If we unleash a restless spirit into this house, do you think *that* will give them nightmares?"

I shivered.

"Are you scared of ghosts?" Dakota hissed.

I didn't think I was scared of ghosts. But I was terrified of the thought of Kitty being restless, caught somewhere between heaven and Earth.

Once everyone else had gone to bed, it was time for the séance. "We have to be quiet," Sydney said, "so we don't wake them up."

"It's almost midnight," Dakota said, checking her phone. "The witching hour."

I felt goose pimples break out all down my arms.

The four of us sat in a circle on the floor of Sydney's bedroom, holding hands. We'd turned off all the lights, so

I could see my friends thanks only to the streetlamps outside and the night-light casting eerie shadows on the walls. None of us had been able to find a crystal ball, but Kianna put a glass of water in the middle of our circle, because she'd read online that spirits could disturb the water to make their presence known.

"Everyone close your eyes tight," Dakota ordered. We did. Then she went on, in a deep voice: "Spirits, we welcome you into our home tonight. We wish to communicate with you; we wish to hear whatever you have to tell us. You are safe here."

I cleared my throat. "Dakota?"

"What?"

"Shouldn't we try to summon a particular spirit? Don't you think that might work better than just calling any random spirit at all?"

"My grandmother!" Kianna blurted out, squeezing my hand. "I want to know how she's doing."

I took on a deep voice of my own and intoned, "Kitty, are you there? It's me. I'm here."

"Who's Kitty?" Kianna asked in a whisper, her hand gripping mine even more tightly now.

"Kitty," I said again, my eyes squeezed shut. "I'm here, Kitty. I'm waiting right here. I want to talk to you. Please, *please*, talk to me. If you're with us, do something to make your presence known. Please."

A moment passed in silence. I felt a cool air, and a quiet rustling.

I heard Kianna gasp beside me. She pulled her hand away from me.

I opened my eyes to see that the cup in the middle of our circle had been knocked over. Water was spreading across the floor, seeping into the rug, dampening our legs.

Then Kianna started to scream.

CHAPTER 17

It took more than an hour for everyone to calm down after the séance. Sydney's parents had sprung awake at the sound of Kianna's screaming and had come running into the room in their pajamas. Once they realized that nobody was hurt, and Kianna was just screaming because a glass of water had spilled, they immediately turned from concerned to annoyed.

"Go to bed," they told us. "It's late."

But Kianna wouldn't stop shrieking. "There was a ghost! This house is haunted!" There seemed to be a part of her that was relishing the drama. But I was furious with her.

Kitty had been here. Kitty had come to see me. And Kianna had ruined it all by breaking the circle and panicking. If she'd just stayed still, maybe Kitty would have told me something useful. Maybe I could have begged for her forgiveness. To Kianna this was all some big game. But it was my *life*.

All the commotion woke Sydney's sisters, and they started crying, so their parents left us to comfort them. "*Go. To. Bed*," Sydney's stepdad said in an I-mean-business tone before firmly closing the door behind him.

But we didn't follow his orders right away. Dakota kept teasing Kianna that the spirit might come back, and it might want something from her.

"It won't," I snapped at last, weary of all of this.

"Won't what?" Kianna asked, her voice extra-trembly. "Come back, or want something from me?"

"Either," I said. "Both. You frightened it away, Kianna, and it's not coming back. Excellent work. Now can we just go to sleep? This séance was a terrible idea."

"No, it wasn't," Dakota objected. "I can't wait to tell everyone that we caught an actual spirit from the afterworld. They are going to be *so* jealous."

Eventually the girls followed my advice, and they fell asleep. It was late, and I imagined they had worn themselves out with all the drama. But I lay on the floor in a sleeping bag and kept staring at the night-light, running through anagram after anagram of anything I could think of, wishing with all my heart that Kitty's ghost would come back for me.

When I couldn't lie still anymore, I got up and stood by the window, looking at the empty street. Other than the slight rustling of tree leaves, the view outside the window looked like a photograph, frozen in time.

"There wasn't really a ghost," a voice whispered.

I turned. It was Sydney, standing next to me, her hair messy from being in bed.

"Yes, there was," I said, but she shook her head firmly. "How do you know?" I asked softly.

"Because I opened my eyes a little and I saw Dakota knock over the glass with her foot."

"Really?" I breathed. Sydney nodded. "But . . . why would she do that?"

Sydney shrugged. "To make it more exciting, I guess. And to mess with us, especially Kianna. Don't worry about it. Dakota does stuff like that."

My heart felt heavy and raw, as if I'd just lost something I hadn't even known I had.

"You really wanted to see a ghost, didn't you?" Sydney asked, looking at me closely.

I shrugged and swallowed hard.

"Did you believe we actually got in touch with a spirit?" Sydney asked, her voice gentle. "I knew Kianna was going to believe it. I'll tell her the truth tomorrow, once Dakota's gone."

"I didn't believe it," I told her, finding my voice at last. "Not for a minute. What do you think I am, stupid?" And I went back to my sleeping bag without saying another word.

On Monday, I was back at the library, looking for my next idea for getting back home. One thing I knew was that I wasn't going to hold another séance. Not with those girls, not ever again. But that wasn't going to stop me from trying anything else I could.

Things kept going from there, more of the same and more of the same. School. Friends. Library. Home. Supper. Washing up. Homework. Reading. Bedtime.

Each night Melanie would tuck me into Penelope's pink bed and draw shut Penelope's pink curtains. I would fall asleep hoping as hard as I could not to dream of Kitty. *Tonight, please, tonight at least, don't make me dream of Kitty.* Some nights this prayer worked. But just as often, it did not.

In the morning I would wake up, and the daily pattern would repeat.

In a way it was shocking to me how little anyone asked about where I had come from, or my life before Sutton. The whole town accepted me as if I had always been there. I think some people—like Miss Timms, and my teacher at school—felt that my story wasn't any of their business. And some people—like Dakota—simply weren't interested.

The one person who did push me for information and explanations was Mr. Babcock. Once a week, he came to the house to meet with me. But over time, when I had nothing new to report about either my foster parents or my real parents, Mr. Babcock's visits dropped off, though he always reminded me that I could call him "twenty-four seven" if I needed to.

That was my life, day after day. Then those days turned into weeks, and the weeks into months, and the months into seasons. And just like that, almost three years went by.

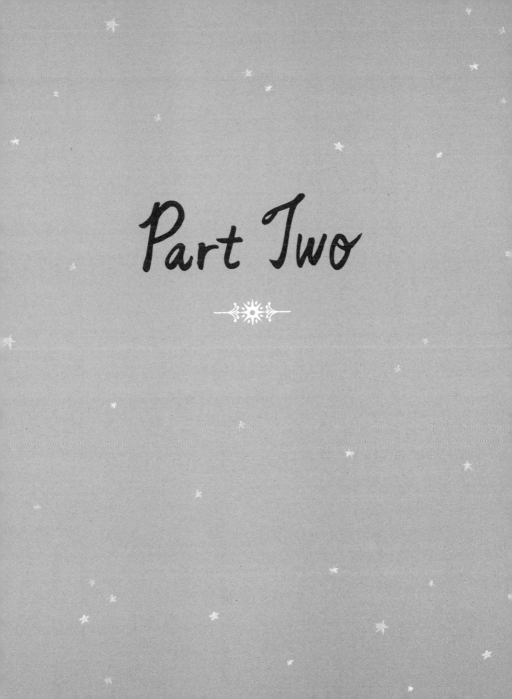

Part Two

CHAPTER 18

The morning of July 18, my thirteenth birthday, I awoke bathed in sweat, despite the powerful air conditioning vent right next to my bed. I pulled myself into wakefulness as a rodent might drag itself out of a swamp—pieces of my dream still clung to me like mud, heavy and slick.

There was a girl. A girl with hazel eyes just like mine, and airy blond hair that framed her face like a halo. *Lottie,* she whispered, her porcelain hand reaching out for mine. *Lottie, don't go.*

I had seen this girl before, in dreams. Sometimes I dreamt of her every single night for a week. Sometimes months would go by without her. But she always came back.

I would have taken her hand—grabbed it as hard as I could and never let go—but I was stuck here, in this swamp between dreaming and waking, and try as I might, I could not make my arm move toward her.

Just tell me where you're going so I can come with you, she pleaded.

But my dream-self said nothing, as though I wasn't even there.

Just tell me why you're leaving me, she whispered. *Why did you leave me, Lottie? . . . Lottie?*

"Charlotte!"

My eyes sprung open. I was awake now, staring up at Melanie. The blond girl disappeared like a blown-out candle.

"Happy thirteenth birthday, sweetie!" Melanie said. "Look who's here to see you."

Dakota, Kianna, and Sydney came running in from the hallway. "Happy birthday to you," they sang. "Happy birthday to you!" Dakota shot a glare at Sydney, who was, as always, off-key. "Happy birthday, dear Charlotte. Happy birthday to you!"

The three of them jumped onto my bed, and we were suddenly a mess of squeals and intermingled limbs and a chocolate chip muffin that Kianna dropped on my sheets, sending crumbs everywhere.

"Ugh," she groaned. "That was supposed to be your birthday breakfast in bed!"

I fished the muffin out from under my comforter and took a bite. "I'll eat it anyway."

"Girls," Melanie said, "let Charlotte get out of bed so we can get the celebrations under way! You all have a busy day ahead of you." She kissed me on the forehead and left my room.

I climbed out from under the pig-pile and started sorting through my closet, trying to decide what to wear. At last I settled on a little cheerleader-esque skirt, a purple tank top, and sparkly ballet flats—a variation on the outfits my friends were wearing.

Once I was dressed, the four of us ran downstairs and outside, where Keith was already firing up the grill. "I hope you girls are hungry for some burgers," he said.

Dakota looked pointedly at her watch and wrinkled her nose. "It's still the *morning*," she said.

"So?" I asked.

"So, it's too early for burgers. You can't eat burgers until the *afternoon*."

With Dakota, I never knew what the rules were until I'd already broken them. I gave Keith a weak smile. "We'll definitely want burgers at some point today," I told him. "Maybe after we come back from the pool."

"I got s'more fixins, too," Keith tried, "since I know how much you love them, Charlotte."

Jake had been right when he told me on the first day of fifth grade that s'mores were the best food in the world. In the nearly three years since that day, Jake Adler and I had not spoken once. I barely ever thought about him, or the time I called him a big fat baby. But I did remember that conversation every time I ate a marshmallow.

"Thanks, Keith," I said. His apron read KISS THE CHEF, but that seemed gross, so I just hugged the chef instead.

Then Melanie emerged from the house, carrying an ice cream cake with both hands. It had fourteen candles glowing brightly: thirteen for me, plus one to grow on. Kianna and Sydney both *ooh*ed appreciatively, and Dakota said, even more exasperated this time, "You can't eat *ice cream* in the morning, either!"

I gave her a helpless look. "But it'll melt if we don't eat it."

Dakota shrugged, like, *not my problem.*

"Make a wish!" Kianna ordered, jumping up and down, as Melanie placed the cake on the little metal patio table.

"What are you going to wish for?" Sydney asked.

"I bet *I* know what she's going to wish for," Dakota said, raising an eyebrow and holding my gaze.

I felt my body tense. "Oh, really?" I said. "What's that?"

Dakota smirked. "You're going to wish for Gavin to ask you out."

Kianna and Sydney both squealed.

I exhaled, my shoulders relaxing. Of course Dakota didn't know what I wished for. How could she?

Gavin Fletcher was going into eighth grade with us. He was nice enough. He was short and his dad was from South Africa, and, according to my friends, this was reason enough for him to be my boyfriend. "You're *also* short," Dakota had explained to me before, as if I hadn't noticed that even after three years of eating modern American food, my body still hadn't caught up with modern American girls'. "And together you guys could have babies with really cute foreign accents."

Then we all screamed *eww*, because obviously having babies would be disgusting, whether they were with Gavin Fletcher or any other boy in all of Sutton Middle School.

The truth was that my accent was less cute than it had been when Dakota first met me. I almost never heard an

English accent these days, outside of an occasional movie or TV show. And I heard so many American accents, constantly, pounding away at my brain. It was easy to forget what my voice was supposed to sound like.

Words had left me, too. Some of those were choices that I'd made, so people wouldn't think I was weird, or ask too many questions. Referring to *rubbish* as *trash* was just easier. Offering to *do the dishes* instead of *the washing up* meant that Melanie and Keith wouldn't look at me funny. But over the years, so many expressions had slipped away from me, even without my choosing. I think I used to say *thank you* differently. There was a different way that I used to say *hello*.

I still clung to my accent, but that was mostly because my friends liked the way it sounded. The other day Sydney asked me if I wanted to watch a movie with her, and I answered *Righto*. That wasn't real. I had never said *righto* when I was English.

Melanie nudged me. "Gavin Fletcher, hmm? Is that the sweet boy who called the house the other day?"

I nodded, staring down at my brightly burning candles.

"*What?*" my friends shrieked.

"You did not tell me that he called," Dakota said, her voice an octave higher than usual.

"What did he want?" Sydney demanded.

"Did he ask you out?" Kianna asked.

"Of course not," Dakota snapped. "Or she would have told us already. *Right?*"

I nodded. "He was just calling to talk. I don't know why. We were only on the phone for a couple minutes before he had to go."

Melanie gave me a wise smile. "He was going to ask you out but he got cold feet at the last minute. Trust me; I saw it a million times with Penelope."

"Just wish for it now and it will definitely happen," Dakota told me.

I gave her a tight smile. Dakota could tell me to do lots of things, and I would do them. But she couldn't tell me what thoughts to have inside of my head.

"Make your wish, sweetie," Melanie encouraged me. "Before wax gets all over the cake."

I closed my eyes to wish, and what I saw there was not Gavin Fletcher at all, but the girl from my dream. Maybe it was impossible for me to ever get her back, or to ever again be the girl who deserved her as a friend. Maybe to believe that those things could happen was silly, childish make-believe.

Yet still, I couldn't help myself. And so I wished, as I did every year on July 18, for her. For nothing at all: just her.

Everyone cheered as I blew out the candles. I opened my eyes, and Kianna snapped a photo. That was Kianna's job: documenting our lives together, creating proof that the four of us were a unit, friends forever, that we never stopped having fun.

Then I stopped smiling for the camera and turned my head abruptly. Because it was crazy.

It was unbelievable.

But I thought I'd seen something out of the corner of my eye. Something in the air, something that shouldn't have been there.

Something that looked remarkably like . . .

A portal.

CHAPTER 19

I'd been wrong.

It wasn't a time travel portal.

There had just been something in the way the late-morning light hit the dust in the air that had made it seem, from my perspective, like something more than it was. But really it was nothing at all.

Of course.

I tried to calm the pounding of my heart and reminded myself that I was just seeing what I wanted to see, and making up magic because I wanted magic to be real. That was all. Because everything I'd tried in the past three years—the séance, the wishes on birthday candles and dandelions and eyelashes, the made-up spells—none of that had made any difference.

The older I got, the more I doubted it all. That I had really lived in England and had a father who was a scientist and had time traveled seventy-three years. I knew what Dakota would say if I told her that story. *That's impossible*, and *That doesn't make sense.* And the more time passed, the more I wondered if she was right. I had no proof of my old life, after all. Just hand-sewn pajamas with a Peter Pan collar, now too small for me, sitting in a plastic bag on the top shelf of my closet. A sad, silent hobby of rearranging the letters in words for myself. And dreams haunted by a blond girl whom I could not forget.

And was that really so bad, if I never found a way out of here? I'd thought it was, but the more I adjusted to Sutton, the less certain I was of that. I had foster parents who loved me, friends to play with, a boy who maybe had a crush on me—it could be a worse life. Did I really need another portal, too?

"Charlotte?" Melanie interrupted my thoughts. "Do you want to cut the cake for your friends?"

I nodded silently, still trying to steady my breathing after the fake portal sighting. My hands shook as I picked up the knife.

"None for me," Dakota said sweetly. "*I* don't eat ice cream this early in the day."

I stared down at the cake and tried to remind myself how we used to celebrate my birthday, when I was Lottie. *Mum would bake me a cake, and Dad would take me to the bookshop and let me choose out whichever books I wanted. Kitty once wrote a pantomime for me, and she got Justine and Thomas to perform it with her, and I laughed so hard I cried. One year for my birthday, before the war, when petrol wasn't rationed, Kitty's mum and dad took us to Burnham-on-Sea and she showed off how fast she could swim and we played mermaids all day long.*

I frowned. That wasn't right. My real birthday had been in October. It would have been too cold to play in the water then. Maybe we had gone to Burnham-on-Sea for *Kitty's* birthday? Or just for a random day trip? Or maybe we had never gone at all.

It was impossible to check these memories. I had no one to ask for confirmation. Even more than my accent, the memories slipped away from me: what Justine wore, how Mum smiled, the way Dad organized his bookshelf, why Kitty's pantomime made me laugh so hard. I would never know.

"Well, *I* certainly want a piece of cake!"

I turned around to see who had spoken. "Miss Timms!" I set down the knife and gave her a big hug. "Hi! What are you doing here?"

Of course I saw Miss Timms often, but only at the library. At first I'd worked at the library every day after school. Then the city council voted to cut back funding to the library even more, so now the only weekdays it was open were Tuesdays and Thursdays. But I still went there every Tuesday and every Thursday after school, without fail, to help Miss Timms with the books. I had never seen her at my house, though.

"I wanted to come wish you a happy birthday, of course," Miss Timms said. "Keith invited me. Here." She handed me a wrapped, rectangular present.

I beamed up at her. It was a book, of course. I knew no one else had gotten me a book. Melanie and Keith always said I didn't need to own any more, since I could borrow whatever I wanted from the library. "And anyway, we wouldn't even know what to get you," Melanie explained. "The way you read, odds are it would be something you'd already finished."

Dakota, Sydney, and Kianna had all chipped in to buy me a makeup kit. They gave it to me yesterday because they were too excited to wait. It had twelve different shades of eye shadow. I had never worn eye shadow, but Dakota said we should now, since we'd be starting eighth grade in a month. I could tell they'd spent a lot of money on the makeup kit. But it wasn't a book.

I opened Miss Timms's gift. "'*The Book Thief*,'" I read aloud, turning it over in my hands. "Thanks, Miss Timms."

"It's by Markus Zusak," she said. "I was concerned that you might not get to the *Z*s any time soon, so I wanted to give this one to you now. What letter are you up to, anyway?"

"*L*," I answered. "I'm doing Madeleine L'Engle now."

Miss Timms nodded. Her eyes were sad. "L'Engle is one of my favorites. I ordered every one of her books for the library. I think you'll like this one, too." She patted *The Book Thief*. "It's so beautiful. It's set during World War Two—"

"Oh."

I felt my lips press together and glanced away from Miss Timms for a moment. I focused on Sydney and Kianna, who had grown tired of waiting for me and started to cut into the cake themselves.

I didn't like to read books about the war. At first I just refused to read any books that I'd read in my previous life.

But then I'd even stopped reading historical fiction set during my previous lifetime. I didn't want to think about any of that. I needed to move on. I needed to look forward.

"Thank you," I said to Miss Timms again.

"You're a great reader, hon," she replied, blinking rapidly. "One of the best I've ever met." She offered me a weak smile.

"Is everything all right?" I asked.

Miss Timms bit her lip, and now it was her turn to look away from me, trying to compose herself. "It's your birthday," she said. "I don't want to upset you."

"Is it Little Furry?" I asked urgently. Miss Timms's pet spaniel was often sick, and I knew he was already pretty old, for a dog. "I'm so sorry."

But she shook her head. "Little Furry is fine. I'm so sorry, Charlotte. It's the library."

I blinked. "What happened to the library?" I asked.

"They're shutting it down," she said. "For good."

CHAPTER 20

Two weeks later, Miss Timms and I were at the library together, boxing up books. This was a tiring process, tiring and sad. I didn't complain, though, because Miss Timms had said, "If we pack the books, then we can donate them to a children's hospital or a homeless shelter or even another library. At least that way someone can still enjoy them. That's how we've gotten a lot of our older books, in fact. The main library in Chicago donated a couple hundred titles to our collection a few years back."

I taped up another box and shoved it against the wall. "Why can't the city council just let the library stay here?" I asked, breaking a long period of silence.

"They redid the city budget," Miss Timms explained, "and decided they just didn't have enough money for it.

When I first started here, there were two librarians, and the library was open from nine every morning until eight every night, except Sundays. Then the council redid the budget, and they had to lay off the other librarian and change the library hours to noon to six. Remember? That was how it was when I first met you. Then the council redid the budget *again*, so the library could only be open three days a week. And then . . . then this."

"It's stupid," I snapped, and Miss Timms nodded her agreement. "Where did all the money for the library *go*?"

"Well, it comes from taxes," Miss Timms explained. "And the city is bringing in less money in taxes now than it used to, for a whole bunch of pretty boring and depressing reasons. As for the money that they're still collecting, the local government decided that other city services needed it more. The fire stations, or the city parks, or the post office, or . . . who knows. They decided Sutton didn't need a library anymore."

"Of course we do!" This was crazy. If Sutton hadn't had a library, where would I have gone on my first day here? Where would I have gone almost every day since then?

"We tried fund-raising," Miss Timms went on. "Some private citizens donated their own money to help keep it open. But we couldn't raise enough money, so it didn't work. And the city council took that as even more of a sign that the people of Sutton didn't care whether we had a library or not. Which is an absurd way of thinking, since the people who most need a library are the ones who *can't* pay for it; the people who need our free Internet and computers and reference materials and a quiet place to sit because they can't afford to buy any of that for themselves."

"How much does it even cost to keep a library open?" I protested. "The books are already here."

"True," Miss Timms said, "but new books are published every day, and I would like to be able to add some of those to the collection, too. And it costs money just to maintain the facilities—to heat the building, to replace broken computers, to use lights and Internet."

"I would work here for free," I offered. "You wouldn't need to keep paying me."

"Thank you, hon," Miss Timms said with a small smile, "but your stipend is nowhere near enough to make the difference between closing down the library or leaving it open. And remember, I make a salary, too."

"*You* could offer to make less money," I suggested.

Miss Timms wiped down a newly empty bookshelf and gave me a wry look. "I don't make that much money to start with, Charlotte. I need to eat. I need to make a living."

"So what are you going to do to make a living now?"

She exhaled for a long time, pressing the air out through her lips. "I don't exactly know yet," she answered at last. "I need to start applying for other librarian jobs."

"But there aren't any other libraries in Sutton," I pointed out.

Miss Timms stopped wiping the bookshelf and looked at me closely. "I won't be in Sutton," she said quietly but clearly.

One of the books I was holding slipped out of my hands. I didn't pick it up. "Where will you be?" My voice trembled.

"I really don't know. I would like to stay nearby, so I can be close to my brother and my nieces. But it will depend on where I can find a job."

"You're leaving me?" I asked, and I could hear my voice going higher and higher, ending in a high-pitched wail.

Miss Timms stepped over a pile of books to come over and wrap her arms around me. "I'm not leaving *you*, Charlotte," she murmured. "I may need to leave. But it is absolutely not because of *you*."

But that doesn't make any difference, does it? When somebody leaves, they leave *you*. Even if you're not the reason *why* they leave, you're still the one left behind.

We get what we deserve. It made sense for wonderful Miss Timms to leave me, because I had left Kitty. So when I cried now, it was not only for Miss Timms or for the library. I cried because nothing in the whole world, no matter how good, can last forever.

"It will be okay," Miss Timms promised me as I sniffled. "I might not have to go very far to find a job. And we can e-mail and talk on the phone. And you have so many good friends here to take care of you! Melanie, Keith, Dakota, Sydney, Kianna . . ."

"They're not the same," I told her.

Miss Timms nodded, and I saw that her eyes were a little wet, too. "I know."

"Now I'm never going to make it to the end of the alphabet," I said numbly. "I was working really hard on that."

"But maybe you can make it to the *Ms*," Miss Timms said. "If you read fast enough. After all, we have the whole rest of the summer before we have to be out of here."

I said nothing. If I knew I could never make it to *Z*, there didn't seem to be much of a point.

"Do you want to get started on boxing up the kids' section?" Miss Timms asked. "That way you won't accidentally pack up anything you're planning to read in the next few weeks."

"Okay." I left Miss Timms and headed over to the children's room with an armful of cardboard boxes. I started with the *As*, since I'd already gone through them all and probably wouldn't need them in the next month.

Stack them up in piles, see how many fit into a box, tape up the box. Do it again. Good-bye, old friends. Good-bye, *Tuck Everlasting*. Good-bye, *Peter and the Starcatchers*. Good-bye, *Tales of a Fourth Grade Nothing*. I hope you are happy, wherever you go.

Then I came to *A Little Princess*. Before throwing it in the box, I paused, looking at it in my hands. The same cover art stared back at me that I knew so well from the Bristol library's copy, seventy-six years ago.

I had avoided this book ever since coming to America, and as I held it now, I knew why. All the memories associated with it came flooding into me: Reading under my desk at school until Miss Dickens noticed and rapped my knuckles with her ruler. Playing make-believe boarding school with Kitty. Getting a new doll for Christmas and naming her Emily, just like Sara Crewe named her doll. Talking about the Magic, like Sara did, as if magic were real.

I sat down on the rug and flipped open the book to the first page. Although I hadn't touched this book for seventy-six years, I knew what to expect.

Once on a dark winter's day, when the yellow fog hung so thick and heavy in the streets of London that the lamps were lighted and the shop windows blazed with gas as they do at night, an odd-looking little girl sat in a cab with her father and was driven rather slowly through the big thoroughfares.

That's one of the wonderful things about books: They are always the same, no matter where or when you are.

But in this copy of *A Little Princess*, something was different. There was a postcard stuck inside the front cover. The postcard showed a picture of a fancy old stone building, with the words HOTEL FIRENZE printed in elaborate script.

I flipped it over. The back side said BENVENUTO DA ITALIA!, and an address was typed below that. This was followed by a handwritten note.

The note was very brief, but it changed my life forever.

Dear Lottie,

I think about you often. I wish I could figure out where you went, and if you're safe. I followed your footsteps, but still I don't suppose I'll ever see you again. I just wanted to leave this note, so you know that you are not forgotten.

Kitty

CHAPTER 21

Kitty was alive.

She hadn't been killed by Nazis in a locked room in 1940, after all.

She had lived.

I stumbled out of the library, clutching the book with the postcard to my chest, calling out some garbled goodbye to Miss Timms as I ran. I made it as far as the park—that park where I'd once eaten out of the garbage—before I collapsed onto a bench. My legs were shaking, my teeth chattering.

I looked through the entire book, page by page, to see if there was anything else different about it. But it was just *A Little Princess*, exactly as I remembered it.

Then I studied the postcard, sucking down its every detail. I hadn't seen this handwriting in decades, but it was undeniably Kitty's. A little neater than I remembered it, maybe, but that made sense; we were older now.

And actually—I tried to wrap my head around the math of it all. Kitty's note said *I followed your footsteps*, but it didn't say *when*. It seemed unlikely that she would have come through the same portal that I did, because then wouldn't she have also landed in Sutton, Wisconsin, in the year 2013, just the same as me? It was much more likely that she had come through a different portal, maybe weeks or months or even *years* later.

And *that* meant that someone must have figured out the secret to time travel after all.

This changed everything. I'd believed that nobody had ever discovered how time travel worked. If my dad couldn't do it, then it couldn't be done. But now it was clear that somebody *had*. They must have done, because somehow, Kitty had figured out where I had gone. And somehow, she had come after me.

My eyes darted everywhere around the park, as if maybe Kitty would be sitting on a nearby bench, waiting for me. But that was silly, of course. Sutton was a small town, and

I had lived here for three years. If Kitty were here, too, we would have already found each other.

I went back to staring at the postcard. It had no postage or "to" line; clearly Kitty had stuck the postcard in the book herself, not sent it through the mail. I wondered when she'd put this postcard in the book, and when she had left the book at the library. Had she thought I'd come to Sutton earlier than I actually had? Did she arrive here in 2010, wait around for me for a couple years, and then leave this postcard and take off?

But if she'd known with certainty that my portal took me to Sutton, then why hadn't she stayed here for as long as it took until I showed up? Did she choose to move on—or was she forced?

The more I thought about it, the more possibilities came to mind, but none of them fit together in a way that made sense. There were only three things I knew for sure, and I clung to them like life preservers in a vast ocean.

One, Kitty had hoped that I would find this note. She had left it in the one book that she trusted I would reread wherever and whenever I was, because she thought that was her best way to reach me.

Two, Kitty had made it out of that locked room safely.

And three, now that I knew Kitty was alive, I would stop at nothing to find her. Forget séances or wishes or spells. I didn't need to contact a ghost or travel backward in time. I just needed to find her in the here and now. I could do it. And I *would*. Even if it took the rest of our lives.

Chapter 22

With as many questions as I had, the only way forward was to do some research and try to find some answers. Unfortunately, the library was now only officially open for a couple hours, only two days a week, as the rest of the time Miss Timms was busy preparing for its closing at the end of the month.

I tried searching for time travel information on my computer at home, as I had many times before. As always, nothing helpful came up. I skimmed through pages on wormholes and cosmic strings, sci-fi stories about time machines, and conspiracy theories claiming that John F. Kennedy or Mahatma Gandhi were actually visitors from the far future. None of this bore any resemblance to my experience, and it didn't shed any light on where Kitty was, either.

But now I knew there *had* to be more out there. Somebody knew something, because that was how Kitty had found a way to come after me.

The next time the library opened to the public was Saturday afternoon. I was getting ready to head over there, to do more serious research than I could at home, when the phone rang.

"Hi," I answered, before adding, as an afterthought, "Hullo." Sometimes I wondered whether any of my friends would even like me if I didn't sound like an English movie character.

"Charlotte?" said the boy's voice on the other end of the line. "Uh, it's Gavin."

"How are you, Gavin?" I asked, searching under my bed for my sneakers. It had only taken a couple months before Penelope's bedroom had become exactly as messy as the room I used to share with Justine. I tried not to feel bad about it.

"Good," Gavin said. "How are you?"

"I'm good." I saw no sneakers, but I *did* find my flip-flops, so I slid those on. I didn't know what Gavin wanted, but if this call went the same as the last one, we were just going to say the word "good" back and forth to each other for what felt like eternity, which to be totally honest I had neither the time nor the interest for. If Melanie was right and he was calling to ask me out, then I wished he would just get it over with.

But maybe I should have been more careful what I wished for, because after a long pause, Gavin blurted out, "Do you want to go to the pool with me?"

I grew still. "Now?"

"Yeah. We could bike over together if you want."

Gavin and I had never spent time together one-on-one. We didn't have any reason to. Before the first time he called me, we'd never even really talked.

I stared at myself in the full-length mirror. Was I really so old, to be asked out on dates, to have a boy care whether or not I said yes? Did I look that old? I didn't feel like I was.

I could go with him, of course. It was a hot day, and a dip in the pool would feel nice. My friends would be impressed. I could easily hear Dakota's voice in my head, telling me that I could start eighth grade with a boyfriend, which she felt was a very convenient way to begin the school year. And even if I spent all afternoon at the library as I'd planned, there was no reason to believe that I'd find any information to bring me closer to Kitty.

But I had survived without her for long enough. I didn't want to wait any longer.

"Thanks, Gavin," I said, "but I'm actually busy today."

"Oh," he said. "That's okay."

"Maybe some other time?" I suggested awkwardly.

"Yeah, maybe."

We got off the phone and I flip-flopped down the road to the library. I tried to ignore the partially empty shelves and half-packed boxes of books as I approached Miss Timms, who was fixing the summer reading display.

"Do you recognize this?" I asked her, holding out Kitty's postcard. I'd found it in Miss Timms's library, after all. She knew a lot about what went on in her library.

Miss Timms glanced at the photo as she rearranged the books, moving them each into the appropriate section of the display. "It's a hotel in Florence, right?" she said. "But I don't recognize it. Why?"

"How do you know that it's Florence?" I demanded.

"'Firenze' is the Italian name for Florence," she explained. "So I guess that's the Hotel Florence."

I made a mental note of that, then pressed, "Forget about the building in the picture. The postcard itself. Have you seen it before?" I flipped it over so she could see Kitty's writing on the back. "Do you recognize this?"

She turned, and her elbow hit a book, knocking over a few others like dominos. She cursed under her breath and picked them up.

"Do you?" I prompted.

She gave a little sigh. "I don't think so, hon. Should I?"

I inspected her closely. Did she know more than she was letting on? Was there some chance she'd helped Kitty hide this postcard?

But I saw nothing in Miss Timms's face that made me think she was hiding anything. Her expression just looked like she was tolerating my sudden obsession with a random postcard while she tried to get everything else done.

"Never mind," I said. "Hey, isn't it almost story time?"

"Oh, jeez, yes!" she said, and she hurried off to gather up the craft materials and picture books.

I sat down at a computer and started poking around the library's database of academic journals. I had never properly read a scientific journal before, but we used to have them at home, since sometimes Dad published his research in them. That was before the war, of course, before he signed the Official Secrets Act, back when he was doing the sort of work that he was allowed to write up and publish.

I thought maybe a publication about physics would help me, but I quickly discovered that there were so *many* physics journals, containing thousands of articles across decades and decades. I'd had no idea there was so much to say about physics, especially so much nonsense—articles with names like "Reassessments of the Boltzmann factor and Brownian ratchets," or "Poynting vector flow in a circular circuit," or "Derivation of the magnetization current from the non-relativistic Pauli equation." Any of these could be exactly the thing I needed, but there was no way for me to tell.

I wished for my dad. He would understand all of this. He would help *me* understand it.

I narrowed in on some articles on the theory of relativity, something called "space-time," the Gödel metric, Stephen Hawking's chronology protection conjecture. All of this seemed like it had something to do with time travel, but none in any way that made sense to me, and I started to wonder why I had thought that reading scientific journals might help me at all. I wasn't my father, I wasn't a scientist; I was just a girl.

A couple hours had gone by, and Miss Timms had made the "half hour until closing" announcement, when I finally hit the jackpot.

It was an article that had been published more than twenty years ago, in 1992, in an Italian journal called *Giornale di Fisica*—which meant *The Journal of Physics,* according to an online translator. It was written in Italian, of course, which was why I hadn't found it more quickly. It said nothing about me or Kitty, specifically—not that I'd thought it would.

But it did mention my father.

It just included his last name, in parentheses, which I knew meant that this article was referencing his research. Breathless, I ran the entire text—eleven pages, each filled with tiny font—through an online translator. The phrasing seemed awkward in places, probably due to the automated translation, but I could still make some sense of it. Well, not really, but about as much sense as I'd been able to make out of any of these articles.

This was what I read, in the paragraph with my last name:

"The now-familiar 'grandfather paradox' posits that time travel to the past is theoretically impossible because, if the time traveler journeyed to the past and were to kill his own grandfather before the grandfather met his grandmother, then the time traveler would not be able to exist—meaning that he would not be able to go back in time and kill his grandfather. To many this has been seen as philosophical proof of the nonexistence of journeys to the past. But if one looks at time as omnipresent, rather than as a straight line of cause and effect, then he can see how both the man and his grandfather exist 'simultaneously, with the difference in years nothing more than a perceived prism, or a curtain that could be, at least for a moment, swept aside' (Bromley 1928)."

Even without understanding exactly what that paragraph meant, or what it was doing in this article, I felt my heart leap. Because there was my father's name, defending the existence of time travel. Whoever wrote this article was someone other than me who knew who my dad was, who had listened to what he had to say.

I muddled my way through the rest of the article. Its name translated to "Theoretical concepts in the space-time continuum." Pretty much all I understood was that this scientist believed time travel was possible, and he had some theories as to how it might function. There was nothing seriously useful, though; nothing that said, "Here are step-by-step instructions to creating a portal," or, "Here is a complete list of real people who have time traveled."

But there was one other paragraph that stopped me. And this is what it said:

"What these hypotheses do not account for is the possibility—indeed, the likelihood—of spontaneously occurring time travel portals. What if a portal were not always a man-made device or machine, but rather an occurrence as natural as an earthquake or a rainbow, only far more rare and localized? What if a portal could simply appear in front of you, shimmering and rippling in midair?"

That idea—a portal that just randomly appeared, shimmering in the air—that was my father's vision of how time travel worked. And it was what had happened to me.

Which meant that the scientist who wrote this article somehow knew *and believed* my father's secret research. Maybe he had time traveled himself, or maybe he'd spoken to someone who had, just as my dad had interviewed that man who saw the portal in Wales.

And maybe the person this scientist had met . . . maybe that was Kitty.

"Five o'clock!" Miss Timms called. "Everyone, please come check out your books. We will be open again next Tuesday!"

Quickly, I printed the article and stuck it in my bag.

"No new books today, Charlotte?" Miss Timms teased as I passed by the front desk. "You'll never get through the *M*s at this rate!"

I shook my head and touched the time travel article with my fingertips. For the first time in my life, books failed to interest me. The only thing I cared about reading and rereading now were those eleven pages.

CHAPTER 23

The author of "Theoretical concepts in the space-time continuum" was an Italian scientist named Dr. Ron Alama. Once I got home from the library, I scoured the computer in the living room for any information about him, anything that might explain how he came to such an accurate picture of a time travel portal.

I found a number of other scientific papers by Dr. Alama, and even more that referenced his work. None of these had to do with time travel. Apparently he had, way back in the 1980s, invented some form of cancer treatment, a radiation therapy that was used in hospitals around the world. There was one photo of him that I saw over and over, showing a distinguished-looking middle-aged white man with a short beard and a big nose.

But he had no social media pages, no contact information that I could find, no information about what university he might currently work for. If I'd wanted to write to him to ask what else he knew, I was completely out of luck. I hated to admit it, but Dr. Alama might just be a dead end.

But I still had the Hotel Firenze.

Kitty's postcard was from Italy. And Dr. Alama was from Italy, too. So maybe Italy was where they had met.

I recalled what my dad used to say: "When something seems like an unbelievable coincidence, then consider that it might not *be* a coincidence."

When Melanie and Keith joined me in the living room for dinner, I closed every window on the computer so they wouldn't see my research and question my sudden interest in Italian physicists. Then I joined them on the couch.

Keith handed me a container of General Tso's chicken and Melanie turned on *Lifeguard Bums*, the new spin-off of *Beach Bums* that she was obsessed with. Personally I didn't like *Lifeguard Bums* any better than I'd liked *Beach Bums*. In fact maybe I even liked it less, because at least in *Beach Bums* there were sometimes dolphins. I often wished I could read during dinnertime, but on the occasions when I had, Melanie and Keith kept asking with great concern what was wrong, and if I wanted them to change the channel, and it wasn't really worth it.

Tonight, though, I didn't want to read. I wanted answers.

"What do you know about Florence?" I asked.

"It's supposed to be a beautiful old city," Keith replied. "Lots of famous art and architecture."

"Michelangelo lived there," Melanie said. "Oh, *come on*," she added to the TV as the guard who was always saying "I must have been a mermaid in a previous life" wiped out on her Jet Ski.

"Have you ever been?" I asked.

"Where?" Keith said. "To Florence?"

I nodded.

"No," he said. "I've never been outside of the United States."

"Yes, you have. We went on that cruise to Jamaica once, remember?" Melanie said.

"Oh, that's right. Well, I've never been to Europe, anyway."

"Do you *want* to go?" I asked. "We could go together! It might be fun."

Keith and Melanie chuckled in unison. "I watched a Travel Channel episode set there, and it definitely looks beautiful," Melanie said. "But it's so expensive, and we already have that great Italian restaurant at the mall, and that's not too far a drive. As for the art, I'm sure it's impressive to see Michelangelo's *David* in person, but seeing pictures of it is nice, too."

"It's so complicated, too," Keith added. "You have to get all the way to Chicago to get an international flight, so by the time you even get on the plane, you'll already have been traveling for hours. And then it's, what, a ten-hour flight to Europe? And airplanes are so uncomfortable these days. They make you pay through the nose just for basic comforts like enough space for your legs, and they place all those restrictions on what you can carry with you . . ."

"And once you get there," Melanie picked up, "how would you possibly get around? I don't know any languages other than English. I guess I might remember some French from high school, but trust me, that was a *long* time ago. And figuring out transportation in those old, unplanned cities sounds like a nightmare. I get lost just when I go to Madison!"

Keith laughed. "That's true, you do."

The more they talked, the better time travel seemed as a means of transport. I remembered that it had made me almost unbearably sick to my stomach. But at least I hadn't needed to worry about leg room.

I used to feel about travel the same way that Keith and Melanie did. When I lived in Bristol and I'd never really been anywhere else, I hadn't felt like I *needed* to go anywhere else.

But now I did.

"Do you think I could go?" I interrupted.

Keith and Melanie both stopped and looked at me. "To Italy?" asked Melanie.

"I'm sure you could go anywhere you set your mind to," Keith replied.

"But, like, now?" I asked.

They laughed some more. Melanie said, "What's the rush?" and turned up the volume on the TV.

After I helped clean up from dinner, I ran up to my room and called Dakota. "I need your help with something," I said when she picked up.

I thought she would be glad for me to ask her. Dakota usually enjoyed it when she got to be an expert. But instead she sighed loudly and said, "Honestly, Charlotte, I'm shocked that you think I'd help you, after what you did today."

My hands grew cold. How would Dakota know about my research today? How would she even piece it together in a way that made it suspicious?

She went on, "Or should I say, what you *didn't* do."

"What did I do or not do?" I asked.

"Oh, please. You know."

"I . . . went to the library."

She shrieked. "So *that's* why you wouldn't go out with Gavin? Because instead you went to the *library*?"

"Wait. Are you mad at me because I didn't go to the pool with Gavin this afternoon?" How did Dakota even know this? Why did she even *care*?

"That was a dumb move," Dakota said. "Why didn't you ask me before you made this decision? Why didn't you even *tell* me? You at least should have done that. We're best friends, Charlotte, and this is one of the most exciting things to happen in your life, ever. I shouldn't have to hear about this news from *Sydney*. It's like you don't even care."

I didn't understand how Sydney had heard about this, either, but that was beside the point. I guessed I could understand why Dakota would be irritated. I remembered when Kitty had gotten her Film Stars invitation, and how upset I'd been that she didn't even tell me about it, when it seemed so tremendously important. If a boy asked her out and she kept it a secret, that would have upset me, too. It would have seemed like she didn't trust me or didn't think I mattered. And technically, yes, Dakota and I were best friends.

But ours was a different sort of best friendship.

Nonetheless, I said, "I'm sorry, Dakota. You're right. I should have told you. You know so much more about boys, so I'm sure you could have helped me."

"And you should have said yes to him," she instructed, already sounding mollified.

"I should have said yes. I think I just got nervous."

"Oh, Charlotte." Dakota tut-tutted. "Charlotte, Charlotte, Charlotte. You have nothing to be nervous about. You're adorable and popular and fun."

"Thank you," I said. "You are, too."

"Yes," Dakota said. "This isn't about me, though. Do you want me to talk to Gavin for you, to see if he'll give you a second chance? I can make up some excuse for today and explain that you really do like him."

"Sure," I said, because that was obviously what she wanted me to say. "That would be brilliant. Thanks ever so much."

"You're welcome! Is that what you wanted my help with? Because I really don't mind taking care of that."

"Actually," I said, "that was just part of it. The other part is, do you have any ideas for how I can convince Melanie and Keith to take me to Italy?"

I'd had enough of Internet research and birthday candle wishes and waiting and hoping and sitting around. Now that I knew Kitty had lived, and had made it into the future, too, it was time for me to act. The sooner the better.

And if anyone could work out a strategy to wheedle and connive an Italian vacation out of my foster parents, Dakota would be the girl for the job. She always got what she wanted. Surely she would have ideas to help me do the same.

But Dakota said, "Ugh. Why do you want to go to Italy?"

"Because . . ." I began, without any plan for how I was going to finish that sentence.

"Let me try again," Dakota said. "You *don't* want to go to Italy."

"Why not?" I asked.

"Because it's not cool."

"It's a country, Dakota," I pointed out. "I don't think entire countries can be cool or not cool."

"Well, you can think whatever you like, but I'm just telling you the truth. Big Fat Baby Jake Adler is going there on vacation with his family."

"Seriously?" I asked. "How do you know that?"

"My mom saw his mom buying a new suitcase, so she asked where they were going. The Adlers think they're *so* fancy. It's nauseating."

"So annoying," I agreed, but I wasn't even listening. Because even though she didn't want me to go to Italy, Dakota had unwittingly helped me work out a strategy of my own.

And that strategy started with Jake Adler.

CHAPTER 24

I biked over to Jake's house first thing the next day. It was odd, being back after three years. When I'd first been here, I didn't know what year it was, or where I was. I hadn't met Miss Timms or Melanie and Keith or Dakota. I was six inches shorter. I was a different person. But here was Jake's big white house, looking exactly the same.

I dropped my bike on the Adlers' front lawn and took a few deep breaths as I stared at their closed front door, mustering up the confidence to knock. I tried to channel Dakota. *Why would* you *be afraid of Big Fat Baby Jake Adler? You're popular and adorable, and he's* nobody.

But even though I knew what Dakota would say, I couldn't make myself believe it. Maybe it wasn't that I was afraid of Jake, exactly. Maybe I was afraid of myself.

I tried some anagrams to calm myself. *Jake Adler. Leaked Jar. A Lead Jerk.* I wondered if he had a middle name. That might help.

I turned away from the front door and slowly walked around the side of the house. *Just another minute, and then I'll knock. Honest.*

When I came to the backyard, I saw an easel set up, facing a big oak tree with a wood swing hanging from it. A watercolor sat on the easel, only half-finished, but already I could pick out the lush green leaves of the tree before me, the texture of the clouds in the sky behind it.

"What are you doing here?"

I turned abruptly to see Jake standing in his back door, holding a paintbrush and a cup.

"Oh, hullo," I said, laying on my accent as thick as I could. "I'm ever so sorry to intrude. I was just looking for . . ." I trailed off.

You. I was looking for you.

Jake kept staring at me in silence, so I cleared my throat and started over. "Is this your painting?"

"Why do you want to know?"

"It's beautiful. It looks so peaceful. I love the way you got so many different shades of green in the leaves."

Jake blinked at me and took a couple steps closer. "I didn't think someone like you would care about art."

"What do you mean, someone like me?" I asked.

He blushed and looked down at his feet. "Never mind," he mumbled. He looked up. "Yeah, okay, I'm painting that. It's just a dumb thing. You don't need to tell anyone, or, whatever, make a whole deal out of it."

"I won't," I said. "Don't worry."

I really did think his painting was good. But I also knew what he meant. Most kids in our class wouldn't care if Jake was a good painter. They would just make fun of him for it, because art was for girls. Which didn't make a lot of sense, now that I thought about it, because a lot of great artists had been men. Like Michelangelo.

"Michelangelo was Italian, right?" I asked.

Jake gave me a confused look, like he wasn't sure how we'd suddenly gotten onto the topic of Italian painters. "Yeah."

"And Leonardo da Vinci."

"Uh-huh."

"Is that why you're going to Italy?" I asked. "Because so many good artists are from there?"

"Who told you I was going to Italy?" Jake asked.

"It doesn't matter," I said, not wanting to invoke Dakota's name around him. "When are you going?"

"What's it to you?" he asked, moving closer to his painting, as if to protect it.

"Just curious," I said. "Just making conversation."

"Look, Charlotte," Jake said, his cheeks bright red, and his words indistinct. "You barely ever talk to me, you and your friends laugh at me when you *know* that I can hear you, and now you're showing up acting all nice and asking me questions about where I'm going and what I'm doing. I might be weird, okay, but I'm not an idiot. I don't know what you're planning this time, but I do know that you're not 'just making conversation.'" He hugged his arms around his skinny chest and looked at the ground.

My cheeks felt hot with shame. *I* wasn't that mean to Jake. There were kids in our grade who treated him a lot worse than I did. Other than that one time, years ago, when Dakota dared me to call him names, I had never gone out of my way to hurt Jake's feelings. I never even talked to him, so how could I be mean to him?

But he was right about one thing: I wasn't just here to make conversation.

"Okay," I said, my voice low as well. "I want something

from you. But it's not to play some trick on you or make fun of you or anything. I want . . . I want to go to Italy with you."

Jake raised his eyes from the ground to stare at me for a long moment. "You're kidding," he said flatly.

"No."

He threw his cup to the ground, splashing water everywhere. His face was still red, but gone was his apologetic tone. Now he shouted right into my face. "What is *wrong* with you? Where do you get off? Do you think you're *so* amazing that you can be selfish and hurtful for years, and then you just get to show up and ask for some huge favor, like we're friends, and I'm going to say yes because . . . why? Because you're *sooo important* that I'd just fall all over myself to do something nice for you? Get over yourself, Charlotte!"

By the time he finished speaking, I was crying. I covered my eyes with my hands, as if that would keep him from noticing.

I couldn't remember the last time I'd wept. I'd stopped at some point. There are only so many times you can cry over the same sadness.

"Oh, come on," Jake said, but his voice was hesitant again. "Charlotte. Ugh, I shouldn't have said all that. Here, why don't you sit down."

I sat on the bench swing, trying to catch the tears with my fingers before they made it down my cheeks.

"Can I get you some water or something?" Jake asked awkwardly. "Or a tissue? This one has some paint on it, but . . ."

"It's okay," I said. "Jake, I'm sorry. You were the first person I met when I got to Sutton, and you helped me. That means so much to me. I wouldn't ask you for help again now if I didn't really, really need it. Please, can I go to Italy with you? I'll pay for my plane ticket. I have money saved up from working at the library. I can do it. But my foster parents won't go with me, and I don't know another way to get there. I will run away if I have to. I will buy a plane ticket and just go."

I shuddered. Starting my life over from scratch here in Sutton had been so hard, the last thing I wanted was to do it again. To go to Italy not speaking the language or knowing the customs, having no friends and no place to stay. If I was lucky I would find another Miss Timms, another Mr. Babcock, another Dakota to take me under her wing. If I wasn't lucky, then who knew what would happen to me.

But I would go anyway. I wasn't being melodramatic when I said that to Jake. Nothing would stop me from looking for Kitty.

"Are you crazy?" Jake asked, looking at me with what I thought might be admiration. "What's in Italy that could be *that* important?"

"It doesn't matter."

"Yes, it *does* matter." Jake sat down on the swing next to me. "If you want me to ask my mom if you can come to Italy on our family vacation—you, a girl she's never met before, never even heard me talk about—then you need to tell me *why*."

"Fine," I said.

"Fine."

He kicked his foot against the dirt below, lightly swinging us back and forth. A few minutes went by while I tried to find the words to explain myself. I would never be able to tell my real friends the truth about Kitty, or about myself. But Jake—well, he was just himself: awkward and embarrassing, immature and wimpy. He never hid any of that. Even if he wanted to, it seemed like he couldn't. And I thought that maybe, to Jake, I could just be myself, too.

But first I'd have to remember who that was.

I started by asking him the same question I'd asked Miss Timms, three years before. "Do you believe in time travel?"

"Of course," Jake said without even stopping to think about it. "Don't you?"

CHAPTER 25

"So let me get this straight," Jake said some time later, still sitting next to me on the swing, after I'd explained to him as much as I was able. "You're saying that you were born in 1930, in *England*, and that first day I saw you, you had just time traveled here—*here*, to Sutton? Who would bother to time travel to *Sutton*?"

"I know it sounds ridiculous . . ." I said.

"Why didn't you tell me all of this in the first place?" Jake demanded. "You are *way* more interesting than I thought you were."

"I'm very interesting," I protested, offended.

"No, you're exactly the same as a zillion other people," he replied. "Except that you're a time traveler, apparently. So that changes things. I'm *obsessed* with time travel."

"Really?" I asked.

"Pretty much any sort of sci-fi, I love. Time travel is great, also intergalactic space travel, teleportation is a good kind of travel, too. . . . Also robots, smart houses, movies where the Internet becomes sentient and starts tearing down humanity. . . . Oh, aliens! Aliens rock."

I laughed. "Do you actually believe all of that could be real?"

Jake's face closed up again, like a light switch had been flicked. "Are you making fun of me?" he asked flatly.

"No! I'm not, honest." I wondered how long it took, how many people had to be mean to you for how many years, before you just started to assume, when someone asked you a question, that they were out to ridicule you.

"Well, if you really want to know: Yeah, I do believe all of that could be real. If not right now, then someday. If one magical thing is possible—like you time traveling—then couldn't it all be possible?"

"I remember when I first got here," I said, "and I discovered the Internet. I thought *that* was magical." A little thrill zinged through my body. This was the first time I'd been able to talk like this to anyone, to admit the truth about why this world seemed so foreign to me.

"Every invention was science fiction at some point," Jake said. "I bet two hundred years ago, there were sci-fi stories with cars and TVs in them, and people read them and thought, 'That sounds great, but it could never happen!' If you can imagine something, then maybe you can make it real."

"I believe that, too," I said. "And that's why I have to go to Italy, as soon as I can."

"Wait, so what exactly do you think is in Italy?" Jake asked.

"Kitty." And I explained to him what had happened since I found the postcard she had left for me in my favorite book. How the postcard was from a hotel in Florence. How there was some Italian physicist who knew about time travel, maybe more than anyone in the world except for me, and the only way I could think that he might know all that would be if he'd met Kitty and she had told him.

"I'm not *positive* that Kitty is there," I concluded, "but it's my best bet. I believe that she left me that postcard as a clue. Kitty loved games and puzzles. She wouldn't leave this postcard just randomly. She would choose a specific postcard for a specific reason. She would trust me to figure it out. So that's what I need to do."

Jake's eyes were wide as he drank all of this in. "But why make it a big riddle?" he asked. "If she was going to leave you a message, why not have it say, 'Here's my e-mail address and phone number, please get in touch'?"

"Because maybe she couldn't," I replied. "Maybe it wasn't safe to do so."

"Not safe, how?"

I shrugged. "If someone could figure out how to time travel on purpose, how it works, that information would be invaluable. You could harness that power to do . . . well, pretty much anything. Kill Adolf Hitler as a baby and prevent World War Two. Meet Albert Einstein and convince him not to tell President Franklin D. Roosevelt to develop the atomic bomb. Stop the assassination of Martin Luther King Jr. The options are limitless. That's why the British government spent so much money trying to figure out how time travel worked. That's why Kitty and I were kidnapped, and why there were people—maybe a lot more people than we knew about—who would kill if that's what it took to get that secret for themselves. And maybe that's why Kitty couldn't just announce her address for any stranger to find."

"But it was years and years ago that those Nazis kidnapped you," Jake countered. "And then Germany lost the war. All the bad guys are dead by now or in jail, I'm sure."

"I hope so," I said. "But if Kitty doesn't want to be easily found, I trust that she has a good reason for it."

Jake shivered. I knew how he felt. I would feel safer with Kitty by my side. I always did.

"So can I come with you to Italy?" I asked.

Jake nodded slightly. "I'll talk to my mom. I'll do everything I can. But here's the deal: If I'm doing this for you, then you have to do some things for me."

"Anything," I promised.

"One, if we go on this trip together, you have to treat me like a normal human being. No name-calling, no taking photos to send to your friends with mean commentary, no judging me for being nice to my mom or whatever. This is my vacation away from people like you, and you are not going to ruin it for me."

"Of course," I said. *People like you.* Did Jake really think I was the sort of person who would do things like that? Just because Dakota and Kianna did, that didn't mean I was the same as them.

"Two," Jake went on listing his conditions. "You have to get all your friends to be nice to me. When school starts, make them say hello to me sometimes. When we're picking teams in gym, they can't pick me last. When they have big parties and invite, like, everyone in the class, they have to invite me, too."

"Absolutely," I promised, with no idea how to make that happen.

"And three: Whatever you find out about time travel," he went on, "you have to tell me *all* of it. Every last thing."

"You'll be the first to know." Then I added, trying to lighten the mood, "Hey, maybe our trip will be fun!"

Jake leveled his gaze at me. "This is a business agreement, Charlotte. It has nothing to do with fun."

"Right." I lowered my gaze. "I'm sorry that I've hurt your feelings," I mumbled.

Jake acted like he hadn't heard. "Do we have a deal?" he asked.

I nodded. "Deal." We shook on it.

"Good," he said. "Now that that's taken care of, let's get you to Italy."

CHAPTER 26

And so began a campaign of intensive pleading, promising, and bargaining. Jake's mom worked especially hard to convince Melanie and Keith. She was a lawyer, so she was good at arguing, and she'd traveled all over the world. She gave my foster parents a whole speech about what an unbelievable multicultural awakening this would be for me, and how safe I would be, and how little freedom I would have, and how strict their sightseeing itinerary was. It worked so well that I developed a new concern—that Melanie and Keith *would* let me go, and then I'd be too busy visiting museums and Roman ruins to search for Kitty.

"I guess Italy sounds nice," Keith said dubiously over breakfast, "but why do you even want to go on a ten-day trip with a kid you barely know?"

"I know Jake," I said, offended. "He's been in my class for three years."

"Sure, but you never invite him over or anything."

"Honey," Melanie said to Keith, giving him a meaningful look, "I think Charlotte has a *crush* on this boy."

"*Oh*," Keith said. He raised his eyebrows like he finally understood everything in the universe.

"No, I don't," I protested, but weakly, because if my having a crush was an acceptable explanation for why I wanted to go to Italy, then I would gladly let Melanie and Keith believe that. "Anyway, I want to try to find my cousin," I reminded him. That was the story Jake and I had told our parents: that Kitty was my cousin, the only family I knew of, and I thought she was living in Florence. It was pretty close to the truth, after all. And if there was one upside to being an orphan, it was that people really wanted to help you find any family you could.

"Let's see what Mr. Babcock says," Melanie decided.

Again I presented my whole case—how I really wanted to go, how meaningful finding any family member would be to me, how I'd saved up the money from my job at the library, how I already had a passport from the time we had driven up to Canada to go camping. Mr. Babcock ran a background check on Jake's mom and turned up nothing wrong with her, so "I think it could be a great experience for Charlotte," he told my foster parents.

And that settled it. I was going to Italy.

"I'm sorry I won't be here to finish packing up," I told Miss Timms on Thursday as we taped together more boxes. "We're flying to Rome next week." I looked around the library. There were still a lot of books left on the shelves, and I did feel bad leaving her to handle them all herself.

"That's okay, hon," she said. "I've never seen you this excited about anything. I understand. Go, have an amazing time, and tell me all about your adventures when you come home."

"Will you still be here?" I asked in a small voice, focusing on the tape gun in my hand. I didn't want to think about Miss Timms finding work elsewhere, moving away. But I also didn't want to be surprised, to return from Italy and find that she'd already left me.

"Oh, yes. The library's official last day is September first. So until then, I'll just be serving the needs of the community as best I can, considering that we'll have barely any books and I can't let them check out anything." She rolled her eyes. "Just what a librarian lives for, right?"

"It's not fair," I said quietly.

"No, it's not. But I just keep telling myself that maybe this adventure needs to come to an end so that a new adventure can begin."

* * *

The next couple of days were a whirlwind of shopping for trip supplies, doing laundry, deciding which books to bring with me, and packing. I was far too busy for anything else, and I managed to convince myself that was the reason I kept avoiding Dakota, Sydney, and Kianna's calls.

But when Sydney messaged me and asked if I wanted to join them for manicures on Saturday, I reluctantly agreed. After all, I'd promised that I would make them start being nice to Jake. I might as well begin working on that now.

At the nail salon, everything seemed like normal, and I started to relax. I shouldn't have been so nervous to tell my friends about my trip. It didn't really affect them, and maybe they would be excited for me, like Miss Timms was.

We spent ages picking out our nail polish colors, as we always did. It wasn't enough just to get colors that each one of us liked; we needed colors that complemented one another, so we could take photos of our nails all together. This time, after much deliberation, we decided to go with rainbow sparkles—so Dakota would wear red sparkles, I would do yellow, Kianna would be green, and Sydney would be blue. Together, a rainbow. I recalled Jake's remark that I was "exactly the same as a zillion other people," and for one wild moment I wanted to paint my nails black, just to prove him wrong.

Kianna excitedly described the various photos we could do once our nails were done. "Like we could stand in rainbow order and each hold our finger over our lips," she said, "like we're saying *shh*. And then we could—"

"Ooh, do you guys want to go into Chicago next weekend?" Dakota interrupted. "My mom said she'd drive us. It would be like one last end-of-summer, back-to-school blowout. We could get tickets to see a musical—wouldn't that be cool?"

"Yeah!" Sydney said. "I haven't been to Chicago in so long. My parents never want to drive that far. And I bet there would be good stuff for you to take pictures of," she suggested to Kianna.

Kianna nodded with excitement as her manicurist rubbed lotion on her hands. "Like the Wrigley Building!"

This was my opening. My hand felt clammy as my manicurist held it, but I licked my lips and spoke up. "It sounds really fun, but I won't be able to join you next weekend. I'm going to be out of town."

"Where?" asked Sydney.

"In Italy." And I forced myself to add, "With Jake Adler and his family."

"*What?*" All three of them leaned in at the same time, Kianna sloshing the bowl of water that her nails were resting in.

"Why?" Sydney asked.

"Because I want to see Italy," I answered. "And I think my cousin lives there."

"But why with *Jake*?"

"Because he's going to Italy."

"When did all of this happen?" Dakota demanded.

"Just a couple days ago. Honestly, it's all been . . . very sudden."

"Are your parents making you go?" Kianna asked, clearly puzzled. "I mean, Jake is just so *weird*."

"Can you tell them you don't want to go?" Dakota asked. "Tell them my mom already got us tickets to see *Phantom of the Opera* in Chicago. That might help convince them."

I tried to explain, as my manicurist started painting the yellow sparkles onto my nails. "Jake's not really that weird, you know. I think he's nice." And I wasn't just saying that because I'd promised him I would make my friends like him. I thought he really must be nice, or else he wouldn't let me go to Italy with him in the first place.

"Hold on a second," Dakota asked, holding up a hand. Her manicurist pulled it back down so she could keep working. "Charlotte, do you *want* to go on this trip with Jake?"

"Yes," I said. "That's why I'm going."

"That's a really dumb move," Dakota advised me.

"I'll be back before you know it," I said. I was surprised to realize that I wasn't feeling nervous anymore. Now I was just feeling annoyed. "I don't see what the problem is. Who says that I can't be friends with Jake *and* you?"

"I do," Dakota replied. "You have to choose."

"Why?" I challenged her.

"Because this isn't just a question about who you hang out with. It's about what kind of person you are. Either you're a person like Jake"—she made a face—"or you're a person like us. And people like us do not mix with people like Jake. We never have, and we never will."

I nodded. Dakota was right. I'd been around decades before the rest of them, and long ago I had seen the truth of what she said: People like Dakota and people like Jake had *never* gotten along.

The task Jake had asked me to accomplish was impossible. I couldn't just tell these girls positive things about Jake and think that would make them like him. Either they would have to change who they were, or he would. And I didn't believe that any of them were up to the task.

"So what do you choose?" Dakota prompted me.

I could practically feel Kianna and Sydney holding their breath as their eyes darted between the two of us.

"I'm going to Italy," I told Dakota.

She shook her head. "I can't believe you, Charlotte. When you showed up here, you were *nobody*. But we took you in, we shared the Top of the Playground with you, we invited you along to everything we did, we told you all our secrets, we helped you with your clothes and your hair. We've done so much for you."

"I know," I said. "And I appreciate it. I really do."

"Where would you even *be* if it wasn't for us?" Dakota asked.

I didn't reply. I just stared down at the manicurist's quick, sure strokes. I didn't know where I would be if Dakota hadn't taken me under her wing. I had always thought that, without Kitty, I was lucky for any friend I could get. But maybe that wasn't true.

Friendships might start as luck, like how it was *lucky* that Mrs. McLaughlin and my mum ran into each other pushing us in prams around the Downs before Kitty and I could even speak, or how it was *lucky* that Dakota was at the mall when I was new to town and all alone. But to stay in a friendship didn't have much to do with luck. That was a choice, a choice that you made and remade every day.

"Since the first day I met you, I've done everything you told me to," I said. "From the very first *minute*, I wore that T-shirt you told me to wear. But I don't need to follow all your rules anymore, Dakota. Because now I have other friends."

"What, you mean Jake?" she scoffed.

No, I didn't mean Jake. Jake had made it clear that he didn't want to be friends with me, that he was only letting me come on this trip because I had things that he wanted.

But somewhere in the world, I had a friend.

"I'm going to Italy," I said again, quietly but forcefully, looking Dakota right in the eye.

"You will never get to hang out with us again," she threatened me.

"If that's how you need it to be," I said, "then that's how it will be." To the manicurist I added, "I'm done here."

I stood up, my nails still wet. And once again I walked out of my old life, and into the next.

CHAPTER 27

Five days later, I was on a plane at O'Hare Airport. My suitcase with miniature toothpaste and new sneakers and ten days' worth of clothes was stowed overhead, my backpack with way too many books was underneath the seat, my seat belt was buckled, and I was ready to fly.

Jake sat next to me, flipping channels on the little TV screen in front of him. His brother, Noah, home from college, was on his other side, engrossed in his cell phone even though the flight attendant had twice told us to stop using them. Their mother sat across the aisle from Noah, reading the newspaper.

I fidgeted with my seat belt and my hair and my cardigan. I tried finding something to watch on the TV, and then I looked through all my books, but nothing seemed interesting. Eventually I just pulled out the postcard from Kitty and held it.

"Are you okay?" Jake asked when my fidgeting accidentally resulted in an elbow jab to his ribs.

I clutched the postcard more tightly. "Is it scary?" I asked.

"What?"

I lowered my voice. "Flying."

"Oh! No, not really. Sometimes it gets a little bumpy and your stomach might hurt for a few minutes, but usually once you're up in the air you don't even notice that you're not sitting on land." He grinned at me quizzically. "You've never been on a plane before?"

I made a face at him. "The only people I knew of who flew planes were in the RAF."

"The what?"

"The Royal Air Force. They dropped bombs on Germany."

"Oh." The grin faded from his face. "This isn't that sort of plane."

"I can tell."

"I thought you said your foster parents had a daughter who lived far away," Jake said. "You've never flown to visit her?"

"Nope. Melanie and Keith don't like to travel. I've met Penelope a few times, but only when she comes back to Sutton."

"Well," Jake said, "compared to being kidnapped, held at gunpoint, and time traveling, this plane ride is going to be one of the least scary things you've ever done."

That relaxed me a little. I gave him a weak smile.

"Is that Kitty's postcard?" he asked, looking down at it with reverence. I nodded and held it out so he could see. "'*Know that you are not forgotten*,'" he read aloud. "Wow. That is so beautiful. I wish someone felt that way about me." He blushed. "I mean, my mom does. But you know what I mean. A friend like that would be cool."

I nodded. "There aren't many of them in the world."

Jake gave a sharp laugh. "Yeah, that doesn't really seem like Dakota's style."

I didn't reply. I hadn't heard from those girls since leaving them at the nail salon. I was so focused on getting to Kitty that I barely even missed them. Still, I didn't want Jake to know that they weren't my friends anymore. If I couldn't help him with Dakota, then what was I even good for?

Instead of saying anything, I just looked at Kitty's words for the millionth time and thought about how her hands had touched this same piece of paper that my hands were now on. If I couldn't find her, this would be the closest our hands ever came to touching each other again. And how could that be enough?

"I owe your mum so much for convincing Melanie and Keith to let me go with you," I said to Jake after a moment. "That was amazing of her."

The plane slowly started to move forward. We were still on the ground, but I could see out the window that we were in motion. My stomach roiled, even though I knew it was silly: What we were doing right now was no scarier than sitting in a car.

"My mom really did it for me," Jake explained. He glanced past Noah to make sure that his mother wasn't listening and went on in a low voice, "This is the first time I invited a friend to do something with me in, like . . . a while. She was just so excited that there was someone who wanted to spend time with me that she would have done anything to make it happen."

I felt horrible. I liked Jake, and the more I got to know him, the more I found to like about him. But we both knew that wasn't why I'd asked to be invited.

"I'm sorry," I told him.

He shrugged. "It is what it is. Noah was so mad, though." He gave a high-pitched giggle. "He was like, 'Why don't *I* get to bring a friend to Italy with me?' And I was like, 'Yes! Years of unpopularity finally pay off!'" Jake did a fist pump, and I had to laugh.

Then I felt my seat tilt back slightly, and I twisted to look out the window and see the ground recede beneath us. Within minutes, the skyscrapers of Chicago had faded to mere specks, dolls' houses, before they disappeared entirely into the distance, and we ascended into the clouds.

CHAPTER 28

Twelve hours later, after flying through the night and switching planes at the airport in Paris, we touched down in Rome. By the time we'd collected suitcases, made it through passport control, and got a taxi to the hotel, it was nearly five p.m. Italian time, which meant that my body thought it was ten a.m. Wisconsin time, and my brain had no idea what was going on. I must have fallen asleep for a bit on the plane, but it didn't feel like I'd gotten any rest to speak of, and when we made it up to our hotel rooms, I was entirely discombobulated, as if I was seeing the world through a thick fog. Everything felt like too much effort, even taking a nap.

Still, I reminded myself, this was less disorienting than time travel, since I'd skipped over only seven hours instead of seven decades.

Our hotel was an old building with lots of paintings on the walls and no elevator. We dragged our suitcases up the dimly lit staircase, and then Jake's mom, Rachel, instructed us to get freshened up and rest a little before dinner.

"I don't even want dinner," Jake said as he fumbled with the big key to his room. "I could just go to bed right now and sleep for a million years."

"We have to get on Italian time as soon as we can," his mother told him. "If you went to bed for the night now, trust me, you'd wake up at three in the morning, and you'd never get on a normal schedule."

"Not me," Noah volunteered with a yawn. "I could go to bed now and sleep until a normal time tomorrow."

"Yes, well, my darling, you are a teenager. You come equipped with superhuman sleep powers."

Jake and his brother would be sharing a room, and I'd be sleeping on a cot in their mother's room. I felt weird about this because I barely knew Rachel and she seemed intense, sharp-eyed and fast-talking, but she'd been very clear that there was one room for boys and one room for girls and that was that.

I used Rachel's laptop to send a quick e-mail to Melanie and Keith, to let them know I'd arrived safely, and then I lay down on my cot, trying to figure out if it was worth unpacking or not. We'd be in Rome for the first four days before taking a train up to Florence—which was, of course, the part of the trip that interested me. If I could have fast-forwarded through the next few days, I would have.

The next thing I knew, Rachel was saying, "Wake up, Charlotte, it's dinnertime."

I rubbed my eyes and looked around. My suitcase still sat unopened next to me. So much for unpacking.

In the cramped little bathroom, I brushed my hair and my teeth and splashed water on my face. Then we collected Jake and Noah from their room next to ours, and we headed out into the streets of Rome.

It was dark by now, but the sidewalks were bustling with people, many conversing in loud Italian, but I also heard English and Japanese and languages that I didn't recognize.

We walked down skinny streets with buildings pressing in on both sides, colorful laundry hanging out on clotheslines above—and then these alleyways would open into plazas (or *piazzas*, as the street signs called them) filled with shops and restaurants. Men in business suits bicycled past us, jabbering back and forth, and I saw smartly dressed women and elderly couples walking around licking ice cream cones. I noticed surprisingly few cars—and those that I did see were more compact than the cars in Sutton—but there were a lot more motorbikes here, in all different bright colors.

It was so odd, because of course I had never been here before in my whole life, but I felt immediately comfortable. As if I was home. Rome felt nothing at all like Sutton. And it didn't really feel like Bristol, either. But this city reminded me in some ways of the place where I'd been born. Things here felt *old*, in a way that Wisconsin never did.

Time. The more I thought about it, the harder it was to fathom. The way it just kept going, and how no two times and places were the same, yet they all had certain things in common, how people have always had homes, food, families, communities, friends.

"Let's eat here," Rachel said. "This piazza is charming."

There was a big stone fountain in the middle of the square, with pigeons flocking around it. A grand old church dominated the view, and the rest of the buildings were restaurants with tables set outside. Jake picked a place with a big sign saying PIZZA, and we sat under an umbrella.

The waiter brought us menus in English, which Noah griped about. "I feel super-condescended to right now. How does *he* know we don't speak his language?"

"Oh, what, do you know Italian now?" Jake asked. "Is that what you're studying at college? 'Cause I thought you were studying frat parties."

Noah shrugged. "I mean, I *might* be bilingual."

The waiter came back a moment later. "What can I get you to drink?" he asked in accented English.

"*Acqua liscia, per favore,*" replied Jake.

"*Prego,*" said the waiter.

Noah stared at his little brother.

"What?" Jake said, opening his eyes wide. "I *might* be bilingual."

I giggled. Jake around his family was so different from Jake at school. I hadn't seen him blush or mumble or stare at the ground once. I wondered if everyone had that: a school-self and a home-self. Like how Sydney was so shy and giggly when teachers called on her in class, but so in-charge when she was with her little sisters.

I didn't quite remember who my home-self was anymore. Sometimes I felt her stirring inside of me, especially when I was at the library. If you close up your home-self for long enough, and you never let her out where other people can see her, does she eventually just cease to exist, so that only your school-self is left—and that just becomes who you are, forever?

We ordered pizzas and salads, and when they came out, I realized that Melanie and Keith had been so, so wrong: Yes, that Italian restaurant at the mall was good, but no, it was *nothing* like this. Everything—the cheese, the tomatoes, the basil—tasted fresher and richer than any pizza I'd ever experienced. There should be some different word for this food. It seemed an insult to call it the same thing we called the prepackaged grocery-store discs in the freezer at home.

As we ate, Rachel talked about plans for the following day. "We'll start at the Colosseum," she said. "Lunch near there, then hit up the Pantheon. We have tickets for the opera tomorrow night—"

"Ugh," Noah interjected.

"I know, going on vacation where your mother pays for everything is miserable, isn't it," Rachel said.

"Operas are boring," Noah said. "Do I have to go?"

"Have you ever even *been* to the opera?" asked Jake.

"Have *you*?" Noah countered.

Jake turned to his mother. "I thought we were going to get to see art that I can study. Is there any art at those places?"

"Look around you," Rachel said, sweeping her arm at the piazza. "Italy *is* art. You want to know why so many great painters and sculptors and architects come from this country, why Florence is literally the birthplace of the Renaissance? Because it is a beautiful place. Open yourself up to it, and it will inspire you."

After dinner, we took a long, meandering route back to the hotel, walking along the river. Across it I could see a brilliantly illuminated domed building, and I thought that Rachel was right: I didn't need to go to a museum when walking through Rome itself felt like walking through a living, breathing painting.

"So what's the plan?" Jake asked me in a quiet voice when his mom and brother had walked a little ways ahead of us.

I was silent.

"There *is* a plan, right?"

"Of course," I snapped. "I just don't think we're going to find anything in Rome. Kitty's postcard was from Florence, remember, and we won't be there until later this week."

"What's the plan once we get to Florence, then?"

"We go to that hotel," I said. "The one from the postcard. Even if Kitty isn't there, maybe someone will know when she was, or where she went. Or maybe she left the next clue there."

It wasn't perfect. But it was better than nothing. And I was glad that, for the first time in three years, I wasn't on this quest alone anymore. I had Jake to strategize with now.

Still, I was desperately aware of how little time we had. Four days in Rome, where I had no reason to believe Kitty would be. Six days in Florence. And then back to Sutton, back to school, back to normal.

This was my one chance. I couldn't waste it.

Chapter 29

The next few days were a tireless march from ancient ruins to art museums to Catholic churches, landmark to landmark to landmark. Jake took a sketchbook with him everywhere and was able to lose himself in the sights, passing half an hour just by sitting in front of a lemon tree outside of our hotel and drawing it in as much detail as he could.

I, on the other hand, found myself unable to be still, continually picking up books and turning the pages, only to realize that I hadn't processed a single word in them. I didn't want to be sitting and taking in the scenery. I wanted to be *doing*.

After four days in Rome, we packed up and traveled to Florence. The train was spacious and fast, zooming through lush green fields and olive groves, with hills rising far off in the distance. Jake and I sat next to each other, munching on panini that we'd bought near the train station.

"I'm so excited to see Florence," he said. "Are you excited?"

"I guess." This tight feeling in my stomach—was that excitement?

"What are you going to say to her when you find her?" he asked. "You haven't seen her since you were, what, ten?"

"I always thought I would ask her to forgive me," I answered quietly.

"For what?" he asked. "*You* didn't kidnap her and try to kill her. You definitely didn't call up any Nazi spies and say, 'Psst, Kitty's here, come get her!'"

I couldn't even laugh at that. "They weren't trying to take her," I said. "They were just trying to get to my dad. I told them she was my *sister*! How stupid am I? If I hadn't done that, they would have left her alone. And when I saw that portal, I should have brought her with me. I shouldn't have just left her there.

"But you know what, Jake? If she hadn't been friends with me at all—if she'd taken the Film Stars up on their invitation—she wouldn't even have been at my house in the first place. Bad things happen when people get close to me. Kitty should have gone with Betsy that night. That's the truth of it."

"Whoa," Jake said. "What are the Film Stars? Who's Betsy?"

"It doesn't matter," I told him. "It's so far in the past."

"Okay," he said. "But none of that really makes sense. You know that, right? Kitty was friends with you because she wanted to be friends with you. You didn't force her into it. And sure, it would have been great if you could have brought her through the portal. But from what you've told me, there probably wouldn't have been time for that, and trying might have gotten you both killed."

I nodded reluctantly. "I've just always felt like I did something wrong by making it out alive when she didn't. That wasn't fair."

"It wasn't your fault," Jake said.

"Who cares whose fault it was? It still *wasn't fair*. But since she lived . . . since we both lived . . ." I trailed off.

"That means you don't need to feel guilty anymore," Jake supplied.

"Right," I said. "And that changes *everything*." I looked out the window for a moment, at the countryside unfurling before us, then turned back to him. "I'll have these moments of absolute certainty, where I expect her to be right behind me in line, or sitting next to me at a café. And then I'll have moments where I think—the world is too big, and we have too little to go on. It's silly of me to think this could work. I need to grow up and get real."

Jake chewed slowly and swallowed. "So, okay, what happens if you never find her?"

"I don't want to think about it."

"No, seriously, what happens?"

I leaned my head against the train window, feeling it rattle slightly against my temple. "Nothing happens. I go home. I go back to school. I find some new extracurricular now that the library is closed." *I find some new friends*, I added to myself. "I keep living."

"So, the same stuff you would have done if you'd never found that postcard," Jake said.

"I suppose. Except that there will be this little bit of time when I had hope. And it's easier not to get something when you'd never even hoped for it in the first place."

"I know," Jake said. His fingers started making little tears in his now-empty sandwich wrapper. "It's like the last time I had a birthday party. It was a few months before you showed up. The theme was *Star Wars*. My mom and I spent ages planning it. She got a piñata shaped like the Death Star and these cool glowing light sabers for party favors." He fell silent.

After a moment, I prompted him. "So what happened?"

"Oh." He shrugged elaborately. "Nobody came."

"Oh, Jake."

"Well, okay, Tyler came. But he was really embarrassed to be there when he realized that no one else was going to show up. And then I was embarrassed, too. It was just like one big embarrassment party. Or one small embarrassment party? Whatever."

"I'm sorry."

"No, no, it was years ago. I don't even care. I'm just saying, that's the last time I tried to have a party, because you're right: It's easier not to get something when you'd never even hoped for it in the first place."

Then he pulled out his sketch pad and leaned over it, painstakingly drawing from a photo that he'd taken earlier of our hotel's façade. I watched him for a moment, but he didn't look up at all.

I turned to look back out the window, at the lush green fields, the blue sky dotted with fluffy white clouds, the low scrub trees, and the occasional village with its red-tile-roofed clusters of buildings. I listened to the scraping of Jake's pencil and the beeping of Noah's cell phone game and the rustling of Rachel's book pages and the clatter of wheels on train tracks, and I tried not to think about how each repetition of those noises brought me a little bit closer to Kitty—or to nothing at all.

CHAPTER 30

After we'd checked into our hotel in Florence, a yellowish-beige building with awnings and big windows looking out over the river, the first thing we did was go to the place from Kitty's postcard: the Hotel Firenze.

"I don't understand why you guys are so obsessed with seeing a hotel," Noah grumbled as Jake and I led the way down narrow, zigzagging streets, trying to find the address from the back of the postcard. "If you love hotels so much, why not just go back to the hotel we're *staying* in?"

"I have to say that I see Noah's point," Rachel agreed, taking the map back from Jake and flipping it around. "This city is filled with art, architecture, history, food, shopping—there's more than we could ever hope to see in six days. Is a hotel really the priority?"

"Yes," I said.

"This hotel's supposed to have great art in it, too," Jake volunteered. "It's more like a museum with rooms in it than it is like a hotel. That's what I read on their website."

"Is that true?" I whispered to him as we hurried around another corner.

"Sort of," he whispered back.

When we finally found the Hotel Firenze, I saw that he was correct. Inside the stately lobby, the walls were covered in paintings, and Jake immediately pulled out his sketch pad to start copying them down. One in particular caught my eye immediately. It showed a dense cluster of small, colorful buildings—pink, green, yellow, red, purple—all stacked together on a sheer rock cliff over a sparkling aqua body of water. It was captivating. Like a rainbow brought to life. The painting was named *Manarola in Primavera (Manarola in the Spring)*, and I thought that if I kept exploring the world after this trip, Manarola in the spring was exactly the sort of place I would want to go.

"Charlotte?" a voice said, and I managed to tear my attention away from the painting. It was Jake. "Are you going to ask about Kitty?"

"Oh, yes," I said. "Right."

I squared my shoulders, turned away from the painting, and headed to the receptionist's desk. Like everything else in this hotel, it was shiny, tall, and imposing. I stood on my toes to lean across the thick wood and ask, "Do you speak English?"

"Of course, *signorina*," she said. "How may I help you?"

"I'm looking for a guest at the hotel," I said. "Catherine McLaughlin."

The receptionist's fingers flew across the keyboard. When she didn't say anything, I tried, "She might go by Kitty McLaughlin. That's her nickname, you see. But she likes Catherine better, I guess. Because of the anagrams."

The receptionist ignored that. "My apologies, *signorina*. We have no guests with that name."

"Oh. Well, did you have someone with that name before?" I wasn't surprised that Kitty was no longer staying here. Disappointed, but not surprised. And whenever she'd been here, I imagined the hotel might still have her phone number or address on file.

"When was she staying with us?" the receptionist asked.

"I don't know."

"Within the past week? Past month?" she prompted me.

"I don't know," I said again. "Can't you just search for her name and tell me when she was here?"

The receptionist gave me a tight-lipped smile. "I am afraid our system does not work that way. And regardless, we do not give out such information about our guests, due to privacy concerns."

"Oh."

A middle-aged couple came up behind me. "*Guten Tag*," said the man, and the receptionist seamlessly switched into German to check them in.

When they left with their room key a few minutes later, I tried another tack. "Maybe you've seen a girl in this hotel before," I said, "who's around my age, and has the same accent as me, and the same color eyes, but blond hair?" I widened my eyes so she could make out the color.

"I'm sorry," said the receptionist, not sounding very sorry at all. "So many guests pass through here, I really cannot say."

"I'll leave you my e-mail address," I said, my voice quavering a little. "And if you see the girl I'm talking about, maybe . . . maybe you could give it to her?"

"Of course, *signorina*." The receptionist handed me a postcard—the same postcard that Kitty had used, but a fresh one, with no handwritten message on the back. "You may write your e-mail address on here," she told me.

So I did. And then, after another minute, I walked away from the desk, because I didn't know what else to do.

I wandered around the lobby, weaving through big potted plants and small marble sculptures, hoping to see a clue without having the foggiest idea what a clue might look like. I found Jake, who was sitting on a pink upholstered bench. He snapped shut his sketchbook when he saw me coming.

"Let's go," I said to him.

He squinted his eyes up at me. "What did you find out?"

"Nothing. Absolutely nothing."

"Huh. So what are we going to do now? Like, what's the next step?"

I rubbed my eyes. My brain felt fuzzy and dull. "I don't know."

"Are you ready to start sightseeing?" Rachel asked, walking up to us and looking at her watch.

Part of me wanted to stick around, just in case Kitty might show up all of a sudden. But the rest of me knew that wasn't going to happen. "Sure," I told Rachel. "We're ready."

We walked a few blocks over to the Duomo. "This is the main cathedral of Florence," Rachel read to us from her guidebook, as we stood outside, craning our necks back to look up at the massive white building with intricate pink and green detailing. Tourists streamed past us, reading aloud from their own guidebooks, which I assumed said the same things as ours, in their own native languages. "Construction was begun in 1296 and completed in 1436," Rachel went on. "This is the largest brick dome ever. And we can climb to the top of it! It's four hundred and thirty-six steps. Are you kids up for that?" She didn't bother to wait for our answer before she took off.

The climb took a very long time, through narrow passageways and spiral stairwells. Every time we came to the end of a flight, there was another in front of us. My legs ached, but at least I wasn't scared of the height or the cramped quarters. Noah was scared—I could tell because he kept saying things like, "*Why* isn't there an elevator here? Is it even legal to have a building without an elevator? What if there was a fire?"

"They hadn't invented elevators in 1436," Jake pointed out.

"Yeah, duh, Jake, I *know*," snapped Noah, wiping sweat off his brow.

When we finally reached the top, I pressed myself to a railing, staring out at the city sprawled below. We were so high up that the wind blew my hair around my face, and it reminded me a bit of the way the wind used to whip at me across the Downs, a long time ago.

I looked out over the tiled roofs, seeing other church spires and towers rising in the distance. In the piazza below, I saw hundreds, maybe thousands of people swarming around like multicolored bugs. If they were Italian or American, old or young, if they were fighting or in love or strangers, I was too far removed to see it.

Suddenly I felt like Noah in the stairwells: terrified, dizzy. I had reached a dead end, and there were so many people. How could I ever hope to find Kitty among them?

CHAPTER 31

As our time in Florence ticked by, my mood grew worse and worse. That overwhelmed feeling from the top of the cathedral followed me everywhere, and I had no idea what to do about it. I felt rotten to my core, trailing the Adlers from one museum to the next with no real understanding of or interest in what I was seeing there.

Jake was the exact opposite. It was as if he grew into himself the longer we spent away from Sutton—he smiled more, opened his eyes wider, stood up straighter. He could spend hours in front of a single painting or sculpture at the Uffizi Gallery as he worked on mimicking the shading and dimensions in his own notebook.

Rachel got audio guides and read aloud from her guidebook so we had a constant running commentary on whatever sights we were seeing. Noah downed as many cups of gelato and espresso as he could and took to calling all the waitresses "*bella*," which he told us was Italian for "beautiful." ("So bilingual," Jake told him. "Wow, you're just so, so bilingual.") Everyone found a place for themselves in Florence. Everyone except for me.

When we had only two days left on our trip, Jake snapped. Or, I guess, we both did. We were in his hotel room before going out for dinner. Jake was flipping through a comic book. Noah was in the lobby downstairs, probably flirting more with the receptionist. And I was sitting on his bed, trying to read a book but really just staring at Kitty's postcard.

Jake gave a long sigh and noisily turned a page. "What are you doing, Charlotte?"

"Just reading," I said. "I can go, if you want."

"No, I mean, what are you *doing*, here, in Florence, in general." He threw down his comic. "You're not even trying to find your friend anymore. You really think you're going to stumble across her by sitting in my hotel room? Of course not. And if you've decided to give up on looking for her, well, that's your business. But then you should at least enjoy being on a cool vacation and stop acting like it's torture for you to see world-famous Renaissance art. You know?"

I stared at him, open-mouthed. "I have *not* given up on looking for her," I said, stung. "I found her postcard, I did so much research, I worked out a way to get to a whole other *country*—how dare you accuse me of not trying hard enough?"

"I'm not *accusing* you of anything," Jake said. "I just think being all sad and looking at that postcard for the mil-lionth time isn't actually making anything happen. Maybe there's something we're missing, and we're not going to find it by moping around."

"Well, yes, Jake, obviously there's something we're miss-ing," I snapped. "And if you know what it is, I'm all ears!" I slammed my book closed. "You want to know something? Kitty and I used to pretend that we were psychic. We would practice reading each other's minds. But it wasn't real. *None of that was real.* If we were psychic, then I wouldn't be sitting here all by myself right now."

"You're not," Jake pointed out. "I'm here."

"Yes, but you don't even like me! You think I'm mean and boring and selfish—oh, and now you think I'm lazy and mopey, too—and the only reason you let me come along was so I could help you learn more about time travel. And now I can't even do that."

"Okay, yeah, I *used* to think you were mean and boring and selfish," Jake said. "But . . . I don't know. You're a lot different than you seem to be."

I shrugged.

"Why do you even hang out with those girls at school, anyway?" Jake asked, leaning forward. "Dakota and all of them. The more I get to know you, the more I don't get it. You're a lot better when you're not with them."

"I like them," I said. "We have fun together." Or we *had* fun together, before they stopped liking me. "And when I'm with them," I added, "I don't have to be alone."

"What's so bad about being alone?" Jake asked.

"You tell me, Jake. What's so bad about it that you would bring me all the way to Italy, just so *you* wouldn't have to be alone anymore? I think you'd know better than I would."

Jake blinked a number of times. "That's mean," he said quietly. It was the first time his voice had gone mumbly like that in days.

We sat in silence for a moment. I picked up my book again, put it down, and crossed and uncrossed my arms.

At last Jake spoke again. "I just don't get why you have to change who you *are* in order to get people to like you."

"I don't think you even know who I really am," I told him. "I don't think anybody does."

And I stood up and walked out of Jake's room, letting his door slam shut behind me.

*　*　*

Maybe I'd thought that fighting with Jake would make me feel better, as if a few of my problems could somehow become his fault. But instead I just felt worse, like I'd doubled my misery rather than halving it. At the seafood restaurant where we had dinner two hours later, his mother said to him, "Do you want to give Charlotte her present now?"

"No, Mom," Jake muttered, staring down at his swordfish. "It's not ready yet, okay?"

"I think it looks great," she disagreed.

"What present?" I asked. Those were the first words I'd spoken to Jake all evening.

He shrugged. "It's just a dumb thing." He reached into his bag, pulled out a piece of paper, and handed it to me. "Here."

I recognized it immediately. It was a drawing of the *Manarola in Primavera* painting that had mesmerized me at the Hotel Firenze.

"Jake noticed how much you liked it, so he wanted to give you a copy all of your own," Rachel said. "Isn't that nice, Charlotte?"

"Yes," I said. It was. It was so nice, I felt like my heart was cracking in two. Here was Jake, being so nice to me, and I couldn't even be nice back.

After dinner, I changed into my pajamas and lay down on my cot at the foot of Jake's mom's bed. I wished I could go to sleep and wake up back at home.

"Charlotte," Rachel said. She'd just emerged from brushing her teeth and putting all her creams and lotions on her face in the bathroom. She had a very long nighttime ritual, I'd noticed.

"Yes?" I said, setting aside the book that I wasn't really reading.

"I've been so glad to have you on this trip," she said. She sat down on her bed and looked at me. "It's really meant a lot to Jake, to share this experience with you. He's a special kid. I know all parents say that about their children, but, well, Jake has a particularly strong personality. He has no talent for bending it to fit into other people's lives, and I say that with love. So it's all the more meaningful to see how the two of you have clicked. I can tell he really values your friendship."

I had no idea what had prompted Jake's mom to say all of this to me right now. It was like she had some second sight telling her that he and I had been fighting.

Or maybe she'd just noticed how little we'd spoken to each other at dinner, and how weird we'd both been about the drawing he'd done for me.

My stomach twisted at her praise. "Thanks, Rachel," I said, "but I don't think Jake really likes me. He just said I could come on this trip as a 'business arrangement.'"

As soon as the words were out of my mouth, I worried that she'd ask what the arrangement was—what exactly I was supposed to give Jake in exchange for what he'd given me. But instead she laughed lightly. "Yes, that sounds like Jake," she said. "That sounds like Jake trying to protect himself." She clicked off the light and said, "Now let's get to sleep. We have one last big day of sightseeing tomorrow."

Within minutes, I heard Rachel's breathing grow deep and rhythmic. But I stayed awake for a long time, listening to the indistinct conversation and laughter coming from the piazza outside our open window.

When I finally drifted off to sleep, I dreamt of Kitty. She didn't look anything like herself, in my dream, but I knew that it was her because I would always know her. She was trying to anagram Jake's name, but because it was just a dream, it wasn't going right.

"Jake Adler," said Dream Kitty. "It could anagram to I See You."

"No, it couldn't," I said. "There's no *Y* in 'Jake Adler.' Is there?"

"Or '*Star Wars* Friend,'" she said.

I tried to count how many *Rs* were in "*Star Wars* Friend" and how many were in "Jake Adler," but I kept getting lost.

"I don't think that works," I said. "I came up with some good ones for him already, all on my own, because you weren't here to do it."

"Ooh, like what?" she asked.

But then I couldn't remember any of them. "Not everything anagrams, you know," I told her.

"Yes, it does," she insisted. "Everything does."

"Not 'Kitty,'" I reminded her.

"Of course 'Kitty' has an anagram!" She sounded offended. And in my dream, she told me what it was, some other word that you could get if you rearranged the letters in her name just right. Some perfect word, and I tried repeating it to myself over and over, even as she and I kept talking, so that I could bring it with me back into my waking life—because it had just occurred to me that this was a dream, and that pieces of it would get lost when I woke up.

But nothing forces you out of a dream faster than the awareness that waking up is inevitable.

"Don't go," I said to Kitty.

"Of course," she said. "I never leave you."

And then I was awake.

I sat up in bed and looked out the window. I didn't hear any people yet, just the twittering of birds, but the sky was gray and I figured it was nearly dawn. I wasn't tired anymore.

I picked up the drawing Jake had done for me and curled up with it in an overstuffed armchair in the corner of the room. Lightly I touched my fingers to his careful pencil lines and shading. Of course this lacked the vibrant colors of the original, but I could still tell what it was. He really was a good artist. And he was a good friend to notice that I'd liked that painting, to care enough to do something about it.

Looking at his drawing made me feel the same thing I had felt for three years, whenever I thought about Kitty, and what a committed friend she had been to me, and what a rotten friend I had been in return. I was used to feeling this way. I was comfortable with it.

I wished Rachel would wake up and talk to me so I wouldn't have to be alone with these thoughts, but I saw she had her eye mask on and her earplugs in. She was dead to the world. I did some anagramming instead, like Kitty in my dream. *Firenze. Zen fire.*

Manarola. A Alarm On. Loan A Ram. Ron Alama.

My breath caught.

Ron Alama?

Yes. Ron Alama. The Italian scientist who wrote about time travel.

Still clutching Jake's drawing, I crept out of the room, easing the door shut behind me. I walked down the darkened hallway to the boys' room and banged and banged on their door.

After a few moments, Jake flung it open. "Charlotte!" he whispered loudly. His hair was sticking up in all directions, and he was engulfed in a T-shirt that read ONE RING TO RULE THEM ALL. "Are you okay? Is my mom okay? What's wrong?"

"We're fine," I said. "Everyone's fine."

His concern faded into a scowl. "Then what are you *doing*?" he asked. "It's five in the morning."

"I wanted to say I'm sorry," I said. "I'm sorry I told you that you were a big fat baby on the playground that time, I'm sorry for everything since then, and I'm sorry that I won't be able to get Dakota and the rest of them to be nice to you and invite you to parties and stuff. I know I said I could, but I can't. I'm not friends with them anymore. And Miss Timms is leaving, so I guess I don't really have any friends at all now, but I have *you*—I hope—that is, if you're willing to be friends with me. I would really like that. For the past couple years, I've thought that we get what we deserve. And—well, I want to believe that I deserve a friend like you.

"I was lying earlier, Jake. I think you do see who I am. And I know that's not why I came on this trip with you, but it's true anyway."

"Okay," Jake said, looking baffled.

"Really?"

"Yeah," he said. "Okay. I never really cared about those girls in particular. I just wanted somebody at school to be on my side."

"*I'm* on your side," I told him.

"Great." He pushed his hair out of the way. "Then who needs them?"

I smiled at him, and Jake smiled back.

"Oh, and since you're awake anyway," I said, holding up his drawing. "I think I figured out the next clue."

CHAPTER 32

A couple hours later, we were on a train toward Manarola. I watched the sparkling, almost impossibly blue Ligurian Sea pass by out the window as Rachel read from her guidebook. "'Manarola is one of the five towns comprising Cinque Terre, which is Italian for—as you probably guessed—'Five Lands.' The towns are all set along the coast, linked to one another by hiking paths. Together they're part of Cinque Terre National Park, which is a UNESCO World Heritage Site.'"

"Okay," Noah said, "but why are *we* going there?"

"Because it's supposed to be really beautiful," Jake offered.

"Yeah, but it wasn't on that whole itinerary Mom made. I'd never even heard of it before I woke up this morning and you told me we needed to be at the train station in forty-five minutes."

"Sometimes plans change," his mom said. "And Jake and Charlotte really wanted to see this place. It's the town where Charlotte thinks her cousin lives."

"But—"

"Noah," said Rachel sharply. "Drop it. This is going to be a beautiful place, we're going to get good exercise and fresh air, and you're having an adventure."

"What if there was more stuff I wanted to see in Florence, though? More museums or whatever?"

"We'll be back there tonight," Rachel pointed out.

"Yeah, but then we have to leave tomorrow."

"You so did not want to see 'more museums or whatever,'" Jake said. "You just wanted to spend more time with that front desk girl. What's her name? Rozalia?"

"Shut up." Noah leaned across the aisle to punch his brother in the arm.

"*You* shut up."

"I suddenly can't wait to go home," their mother said with a dramatic sigh.

I just kept watching out the window, the cliffs passing us by on one side, the ocean on the other, willing our train forward. We passed into darkness, and I knew that meant we were now going through a tunnel, burrowing our way right through those lush green mountains.

"So what?" Jake had said when I told him, at five in the morning, that the letters in the town name "Manarola" could be rearranged to spell "Ron Alama." "There's an Italian scientist whose name has the same letters as an Italian town. What do you think it means?"

"I think," I told him, "that Dr. Ron Alama was Kitty's way of telling us to go to Manarola."

Okay, so Kitty and I weren't psychic in the Zener card way. We couldn't tell exactly what each other was thinking all the time. Okay, that was just a childish fancy. Yet I believed that we were tied together somehow, that maybe we could communicate across time and space in a manner that wasn't telepathy, but that still felt magical.

Jake's eyes grew bigger and bigger as we stood there in the hotel hall. "Are you sure?"

I hesitated before answering. "No. I'm not sure at all. I don't understand it. But I know what my dad would say if he were here: It seems too unbelievable to be a coincidence."

And that was enough for Jake. "All right," he'd said. "Let's wake up my mom and tell her we need to go."

"Right now? Are you sure?"

"We go home tomorrow. I don't think we can wait."

Now, as Jake and Noah bickered beside me, the train emerged from the tunnel and suddenly I saw it before us: a mishmash of tightly packed little houses in every bright color, clustered together, facing the sea.

Manarola.

CHAPTER 33

"This seems like one of those small towns where everyone knows everyone," Rachel said as we sat at an outdoor café close to the train station, sipping from glass bottles of Fanta and watching shopkeepers bustling around. Laundry hung from clotheslines outside nearly every window, while cats wove their way around tables and rolled around on the stones, warming themselves in the bright sun. Jake kept popping out of his seat to chase down a particularly fluffy and antisocial calico.

I saw a lot of other tourists, mostly hikers with walking sticks and water bottles, but I thought that Rachel was right, and most people who actually lived here would know most everyone else. There just weren't that many houses before the town gave way to the mountains or the sea. And I saw no cars. The only way in or out was to get back on that train. Or to get on a boat, I guessed.

A waiter approached our table and asked, "What can I get you?"

Rachel removed her sunglasses and beamed up at him. "How long have you lived here?"

"Forty years, *signora*," he replied with a little bow.

"Perfect," she said. "Then do you know someone who lives here named . . . Charlotte, what is your cousin's name?"

"Catherine McLaughlin," I supplied. "She's around my age, and she's English, too. She has the same accent as me."

The waiter shook his head. "I am not familiar with anyone of that name. You are sure she lives here, yes? Many people from all across the world visit Cinque Terre. But people who live here, mostly we are Italian. Here it is very, how you say, isolated. You see this, I'm sure. It is not like Milan or Rome. This is not a place where foreigners stay for a long time. You understand?"

"We do, thank you," Rachel assured him.

"Thank *you*, *signora*. And to eat?"

Rachel ordered a tuna salad for herself and for Jake, who was still off chasing cats, and Noah ordered the catch of the day. I ordered a pastry because the waiter wouldn't leave until I said something, but with the tightness in my stomach, I couldn't imagine eating it.

"We can ask other locals after we eat," Rachel assured me. "I'm sure someone will know her."

Even if people didn't know Kitty's name, I thought they would notice if a random English girl with no parents had moved to town. Wouldn't they? A lot of people in Sutton had noticed *me*, and Sutton was much bigger than Manarola.

But we asked a number of people—shopkeepers and fishermen and even some kids around my age. "She goes by Catherine or Kitty," I explained. "She has hazel eyes just like mine, and blond hair. She's fair-skinned and very good at word games." Nobody had seen anyone like that. Or maybe they just didn't speak English fluently enough to understand what I was looking for.

As we got closer to the harbor—a rocky little inlet with some small boats resting on shore and others docked in the water—we saw more and more people. At first I assumed they were tourists taking photos, as we ourselves were doing—how could you not? But then I noticed that the water was filled with swimmers, and many of the people standing ashore were cheering them on, and snapping photos of *them*, not of the gorgeous landscape after all.

"What's going on?" Rachel asked a guy who looked to be a little bit older than Noah, who was whooping and jumping up and down as he watched the water. "Is it a swimming race?"

"Not a race, exactly," he replied in an Italian accent, not taking his eyes off the swimmers. "There are no prizes. It is the Miglio di Manarola. Anyone in good health can swim in it, so many people do!"

"The Manarola Mile?" Jake guessed, and the guy nodded eagerly.

"Stop acting like you understand Italian," Noah muttered to his brother. "Show-off."

"Well, it would seem like I *do* understand Italian," Jake pointed out.

"It starts here in Manarola," the guy went on, "and follows la via dell'Amore down to Riomaggiore. It is not a very far distance, but you must be a good swimmer!"

A mile sounded far to me—I'd never swum more than two laps in the pool without needing to take a break.

"Via dell'Amore," Jake repeated. "The Street of Love?"

"*Stop*," Noah moaned. "I knew that one anyway."

"Oh, right," Jake said. "How could I forget you are a total love expert now?"

I grinned. Since we'd made up this morning, Jake had seemed so confident as to be almost cocky—as if now that he officially had a friend, nothing could keep him down.

Rachel thanked the Italian guy, who hollered, "*Vai, Aldo, vai!*" out at the swimmers, punching his fist in the air. The sea crashed dramatically on the rocks before us, and the spectators standing closest to the edge laughed and sputtered as the water hit them.

"Do you think Kitty might be here somewhere, watching this?" Jake asked me quietly, looking around at the crowds.

I shook my head. "If there's a swimming event that anyone can participate in," I said, "and if Kitty is really here, then I doubt she'd be watching it. She'd probably be *in* it."

"Really?" Jake asked. "How do you know?"

"I don't," I said. "I don't know anything. But Kitty loved swimming. Even her obituary mentioned it," I added bitterly. "I can't imagine her sitting back and watching something like this when she could dive right in herself."

"So how do we find her?" Jake asked. "If you think she's in the water right now—it's not like I'm going to jump in and swim up to everyone and say, 'Excuse me, sorry to interrupt your breaststroke, but are you Kitty?'"

"I think we go to the finish line," I said, "and we watch them get out of the water."

"And if she's not there?" Jake asked.

"Then we're no worse off than we are now."

We told Rachel and Noah the plan, and Noah said, "Whatever," and Rachel said, "I'd love to walk the via dell'Amore. That's a terrific idea. I read about it in the guidebook on the train ride here."

So we started to follow the trail. It wasn't hard to find, since so many people were walking along it, many clearly tourists, others there to cheer on their swimming friends below. It got crowded, so tourists would squeeze past one another saying "Excuse me" in their own languages: "*Excusez-moi*," "*Entschuldigung*," "*Desculpe*," and, of course, the Italian "*Permesso*." I kept staring over the walkway's railing at the colorful swim caps bobbing below, imagining as hard as I could that one of them belonged to the girl I knew.

The path was surrounded by flowers, ferns, cacti, and palm trees. Butterflies flitted through the air before us, as if guiding our way forward, while tiny green lizards darted off the path and disappeared into the thick vegetation. Seagulls cawed overhead.

Jake was captivated. He started keeping a running tab of every color as he spotted it in a flower. We hadn't walked that far before he had completed a rainbow. "This is even better than it looked in that painting," he said. "I think it's the most beautiful place I've ever been in my whole life."

It was the most beautiful place I had ever been, too. And I wondered whether maybe that was the whole reason Kitty had lured me here: maybe not to find her at all, but just so I could see how much majesty the world had to offer.

"What are all those locks doing here?" Noah asked. Thousands of padlocks were affixed to the railing between the path and the sea, to the netting keeping back rocks overhead, and to pretty much anyplace else that a padlock might fit. Some of them had names engraved or handwritten on them—"Matthew + Ame," for example—or little expressions of devotion.

"Let's see what the guidebook says," Rachel replied, pulling us aside so that the other hikers could pass.

"Noooo," Noah groaned. "The guidebook is so boring. I'm sorry I asked."

"It says that closing a lock with your loved one here on the Lovers' Way is a symbolic gesture of securing your love forever. Like carving your names into a tree used to be, I suppose. Now, was that boring?"

"Yes," Noah said, squinting his eyes shut.

"Are you going to put on a padlock for you and Rozalia?" asked Jake with delight.

"I don't know—are you going to put on a padlock for you and *nobody*?"

I ran my fingers over the metal locks hanging overhead, studying the names and phrases on them. I wondered if Kitty really was here, if she would have left a padlock with our names. I didn't see one. But that didn't mean it didn't exist. We kept walking, slowly, with me inspecting as many of them as I could.

When we saw an opportunity to turn onto a less crowded path, we took it. I could still see the swimmers from here—in fact, it was easier, without so many other tourists getting in my way—but this path was steeper, with long sets of stone stairs leading up into the mountainside. It wasn't long before all of us were huffing and puffing.

"I don't know how anyone who lives here manages to carry their groceries home," Rachel gasped out with a laugh.

I thought maybe that was why so few people *did* live out here, far from the town center. The only hint of civilization we saw was farmland—until, out of the blue, we saw a sign that said BAR. We climbed the twisty path behind it, and what do you know—there was a bar.

"That's so random," Jake said, snapping a photo.

"I'm going to buy a beer," Noah said.

"No, you are not," said their mother. Instead she bought us all sparkling waters, and I finished mine in one gulp. The August sun was now high overhead, and the sea breeze wasn't doing enough to wick away the sweat gathering on my forehead and lower back.

We set back out, but somehow the path was still climbing higher. The swimmers were mere specks in the distance now. "Can we sit down for a while?" Jake asked a few minutes later. "My legs hurt."

"That's because you don't get enough exercise," his brother told him.

"And you do? Like playing video games all summer has given you just such well-defined muscles?"

In response, Noah held up his arm and made a fist.

"I don't see anything," Jake said. "Are you flexing? That can't be the best muscle you get when you *flex*."

"Boys," their mother said tiredly.

"Hey, look," Jake said. "There's another sign ahead. Maybe it's another bar and maybe this one will have actual chairs in it. And a bathroom."

We approached the sign, set among the trees, but this one did not say BAR.

It said WILLS TOWER.

"Maybe that's the name of a restaurant?" Jake suggested.

"I don't think they have *restaurants* in the middle of the woods," Noah said.

"Yeah, well, you didn't think they had a *bar* in the middle of the woods, either," Jake said.

"It's not a restaurant," I said. "And it's not a bar. It's the next clue."

They both fell silent.

"Clue?" Noah asked at last.

"To finding Kitty." I felt like everything about me, even my very skin, was vibrating in anticipation.

"How can you tell?" Jake asked.

"Because this is where we said we'd meet. If the war ever separated us, this was where we would find each other again."

"What war?" asked Rachel with concern.

"You said you'd find each other *here*, in the middle of the woods?" Noah asked.

"No," I said. "At Wills Tower."

And then I couldn't discuss it with them anymore. I pounded up the narrow path marked by the sign, up the wooded hill, toward whatever I might find there.

A little house. That's what I found. A stone house with dark green shutters covering its windows, surrounded by trees on all sides. No one would know it was here if they hadn't seen the sign.

I started toward the front door, then turned around when I heard the Adlers still behind me. "Please don't come with me," I said.

Rachel frowned. "Of course we're going to come."

I shook my head.

"Plus," Jake said, "you promised . . . you know."

"I will tell you every single thing I find out," I told him. "But please don't come with me. I need to do this alone."

"I'll make you a deal," Rachel said. "We'll hang back here while you knock. And if anyone other than your cousin opens the door, we're going to join you immediately. Fair?"

"Fair." My chest felt tight, and I was struggling for air. I tried to mop up the perspiration on my face. Then I walked forward, one foot in front of the other, and in all those miles and all those years I had spent separated from Kitty, those last few steps felt like the longest of all.

I banged the door as hard as I could, in the pattern Kitty would know. *Slow. Slow. Fast-fast-fast-fast-fast.*

A minute passed. Then another. And just when I had started to think this wasn't right, this was all just a series of coincidences, the Florence postcard and the Manarola anagrams and all of it—the door opened.

It was her.

"Lottie," she said.

And we fell into each other's arms.

CHAPTER 34

"How old are you?" I asked, at the same moment that Kitty asked me, in pretty much the same astonished tone of voice, "How did you ever find me?" We both laughed a little.

"You first," I said.

"Eighty-six," Kitty replied. "I'm eighty-six years old. I . . . I'm overwhelmed. How are you here? How is this possible? Is this really happening, or am I dreaming?"

"I've dreamt about this so many times," I said. "This time it's different. This time it's real."

We were still holding each other, as if time and space might once again tear us apart if we let go. Finally Kitty pulled back, her eyes shining, and said, "Here, Lottie, come inside."

And at hearing her say my name, *Lottie*, I almost started to bawl. I didn't know how I'd forgotten for so long who I was, when Kitty always knew.

I waved at the Adlers to let them know that I was safe, then followed Kitty into her house. Her steps were slow and deliberate, her back hunched over. No longer was she three inches taller than I, and her wispy blond hair had turned even wispier, and white. But when she turned to look at me, to soak in my physical appearance in the same way that I was taking in hers, I could see that her eyes were exactly the same. The same as they'd always been, the same as mine.

Eighty-six. "How did you get so old?" I asked.

"The same way everybody gets old," she replied. "Time passed. I grew up. How did you get *here*?"

"Oh. That's a really long story," I said.

We sat down next to each other on a sofa in her living room. The room was small but cozy, peaceful, with fascinating decorations—woven wall hangings and artsy photographs and carved statuettes. I saw no TV, no computer, no obvious links to the outside world. I thought that Jake would love it in here: It was like a miniature, personal art museum.

Kitty took my hands in hers. "And how old are *you*?" she asked.

"Thirteen."

Her eyes widened. "So it's been only three years since the last time you saw me?"

Only. I never would have said *only* about those three years. "Yes," I told her, "but it felt a lot longer than that."

"Lottie," she said, the name again sending a thrill down my spine, "I've not seen you in *seventy-six years.* I thought I was never going to see you again."

"I thought *I* was never going to see you again! I thought they killed you."

"I thought you'd time traveled to—well, I had no idea! The fourteen hundreds or the twenty-third century or goodness knows when. Never did I let myself imagine that you might have gone to a day and an age when I would be alive to see you again."

I blinked at her. "But if you thought that I'd wound up hundreds of years ago, or hundreds of years in the future, then why did you leave me all those clues to find you?"

She tilted her head to the side. "What clues?"

"Like this postcard." I pulled it out of my bag and showed it to her. At this point the postcard was looking a little dirty, and a little ragged around the edges, just from how much time I'd spent holding it.

She looked at the photo, then flipped it over to read the message on the back. "Where did you come across this?"

"In the copy of *A Little Princess* at the Sutton library. Isn't that where you put it?"

She shook her head slightly. "Sutton. Where is that?"

Kitty was old. Her wrinkled hands trembled as she held the postcard. I wondered whether perhaps she was so old that she had just . . . forgotten. Forgotten about Sutton, forgotten that she had left a series of clues so that I, and no one else, would be able to find her. And the idea devastated me: that I could finally, finally find Kitty again, but she still wasn't the Kitty I remembered.

"Sutton is a town in Wisconsin, America," I told her slowly, loudly, as I might speak to any elderly person. "It's where I live."

Kitty laughed a little. "Ah. So you're American now?"

"I guess so. I have an American passport."

"And you traveled all the way from America to here . . . because of this postcard?"

I wanted to stomp my feet on the floor. I wanted to throw one of her intricately crafted little statues and shatter it against the wall. I wanted to shake my best friend right out of this old, forgetful, confused lady. "Yes! That was the point of it, Kitty. That's why you put the postcard in the book in the first place, so I could find it and then find you. Remember?"

She was shaking her head again. "I remember many, many things, Lottie, but that is not how it happened." Her voice was authoritative, and I felt myself relax a tiny bit. "Do you want to know what happened?"

"Of course!"

"Good. But first, I'm going to get us something cold to drink. It's such a hot day, isn't it?"

I followed her into her kitchen while she poured us each a glass of sparkling water, and then I followed her back to the sofa. I didn't want to let her out of my sight for an instant.

"I'll start right when you left me." Kitty paused, and I pictured her rewinding the long film of her life all the way back to that day in 1940. "I've never discussed this with anybody," she said, "so forgive me if it comes out wrong.

"We watched you vanish through that portal, and then seconds later the portal vanished, too. It was extraordinary. It was nothing short of magical. Even for Rob—your father, I mean—who had modeled and studied this for so long, who knew every theorem and equation behind what had just happened. . . . Even knowing all that science, it still seemed inexplicable.

"I've had that experience many more times in my life. The first time humans traveled into outer space, the first time I sent an e-mail, or even sometimes when I just look at the stars here in Manarola, I think, *How can this be possible?* But I have never felt that so strongly as the day I watched you disappear into thin air."

I licked my lips and asked, "Were you mad at me for leaving?"

"In that moment? Absolutely not. Lottie, you saved my life by going through that portal. It was the perfect demonstration to make our captors realize, *Yes, time travel really does exist; we have witnessed it with our own eyes.* It gave your father the upper hand. He told them that if they let me live, he would study the portal that had just appeared, he would work out where you went and how you got there. Of course they agreed. This was far more important than my little life."

I scrunched up my face. "That's not true. Nothing's more important than your life."

"Well, I'm just telling you what they thought. It was chaos when you left. Absolute chaos. And those people who had taken us, the people holding us in that room—"

"I remember them." I shuddered. "I never forget them."

"Well, they made a grave error in that moment of panic and confusion. They revealed who they really were."

"What do you mean, 'who they really were'? Weren't they Nazis?"

Kitty sighed. "I wish they had been. The entire rest of my life would have been so much simpler. No, Lottie: They were part of the British Directorate of Military Intelligence."

CHAPTER 35

I nearly knocked over my water glass. "That woman in the gray coat—those men with the guns—they really *were* British? Why on earth would *they* kidnap us? And threaten to *kill* us?! They were supposed to be the good guys! That doesn't make any sense."

"Here's the thing I've realized about war, Lottie," Kitty said, locking eyes with me. "And I have lived through a lot of wars, so by this point I should know. There may be one side that's fighting for freedom and democracy and tolerance, while the other side is fighting for oppression and conformity and fear. There may be one side whose values you agree with, and one side whose values you deplore. In that regard, there may well be 'good guys' and 'bad guys.' But both sides, regardless of what they're fighting *for*, will fight dirty. Both sides will kill people—lots and lots of people—before a war is won."

"Even so," I said, "I don't understand why the British Military Intelligence department thought that kidnapping two little girls would help them win the war."

Kitty nodded; she hadn't understood it at first, either. But, she told me, she and my dad quickly figured out that the British military believed he *had* discovered the secrets of time travel. They believed that he *did* know how to create a portal to a specific time and place, and he just wasn't telling them—maybe for his personal gain, or because he didn't believe the military should be able to use this information.

It was as if a scientist had figured out how to make the atomic bomb, but was refusing to hand over his work to the United States government, and was feigning ignorance so they would not be able to create one of these bombs and drop it on Japan. That's what the British military thought was happening with my dad. So they captured me and Kitty in order to try to force the issue.

"Unfortunately for them," Kitty said, "their plot back-fired enormously."

"What did you do when you realized they weren't Nazis?"

"Oh, your father was livid, naturally. They really would have murdered us—us, loyal British subjects! And even though they didn't, thank goodness, we lost *you*. Your father hoped and prayed that you'd gone someplace where you'd be safe and well cared-for, but he had no way of knowing. He was so worried. He never stopped worrying about you, for the rest of his life."

I blinked back tears. "I *did* go someplace safe. I have been cared for—*so* well cared-for. I didn't know Daddy would be so concerned. He was always so busy and distracted. He didn't seem to really care about my safety or who was taking care of me when I lived under his own roof."

"Once you were gone," Kitty said, "he realized that. He regretted it deeply. You were his daughter, after all. Like many scientists, he lacked some of the skills for showing his feelings, but he loved you desperately."

"I wish there'd been some way to let him know that I was safe."

"I think he sensed it, deep down. Or maybe he just had to believe it, to find any sort of peace."

"So what did you do?" I asked, leaning forward. "When you discovered that our kidnappers were actually part of Military Intelligence, I mean. Did you tell . . ." I tried to imagine who you should tell, when your own military turns on you. "The prime minister?" I tried.

"We didn't know who in the government was part of this plot," Kitty said. "We didn't know who had authorized the whole scheme, or whom we could trust. And it wasn't as though we could just waltz out of the building where we were being held. Not only did they intend to keep us there until your father worked out all the science behind time travel, but also they worried that we *would* tell someone if they released us. Maybe not the prime minister, but the newspapers. Can you imagine how bad that would have looked for Britain's war efforts, if word got out that they were experimenting in time travel, capturing scientists, and shooting at children?"

"Yes," I said. "I absolutely can." Despite the heat, I shivered.

Kitty must have noticed, because she took my hand and held it in hers. Immediately I felt myself relax. "It's okay," she soothed me. "We all made it through safely. It's okay."

I nodded and let out a deep breath. "How *did* you make it out?"

"We kept believing that someone would find us, and rescue us. But weeks passed by, and nobody did. We assumed that our families and perhaps the police were searching but having no success, that we'd been too well hidden. We weren't allowed outside. They put me in a room with a cot and they fed us three times a day, but there were no windows. I was frightened, but I also remember being so *bored*. One of the guards took pity on me and brought me crossword puzzles, but that hardly made up for a lack of sunlight, fresh air, conversation, other children.

"I started hanging around your father in the laboratory they had set up for him, and he would give me little tasks to do—sorting papers or washing beakers, that sort of thing, just to keep me occupied.

"Much later, after we were free, we learned that the reason why nobody rescued us wasn't even because we were so well hidden, but probably because they weren't even searching."

"Why not?" I demanded. "There's no way your parents weren't desperate to find you. They were obsessed with you."

Kitty laughed, maybe a little sadly. "I love that you remember that," she said. "I love talking to someone who remembers my parents." She rubbed her hands over her face. "A statement had been released that your father had taken me and you for an evening stroll, and we'd walked right off the dock and drowned."

"Who would have possibly believed such a story?" I asked with a laugh. "You're an excellent swimmer, and anyway, why would the three of us have been so silly and blind as to wander into the river at night?"

"Not blind," Kitty said, "just unaccustomed to the blackout."

My laughter died instantly. I remembered now how dark Bristol got during the Blitz at night. How any light would just serve to alert the Luftwaffe to the location of the city, to turn our town into a sitting target.

Some people really had been hit by cars whose drivers couldn't see them, they really had broken ankles by walking straight into invisible curbs or trees, and they really had walked off the edge of the dock and into the River Avon. I'd forgotten about this, because I hadn't known any of those people personally, and, considering the more screamingly obvious threats of bombs and fires, the dangers of the blackout seemed much less dramatic.

But apparently everyone who'd known me had thought that I *was* one of those people. Now I understood what those obituaries meant when they referred to *a blackout incident.*

"So that's what your parents and my mum and everyone thought happened to us?" I asked Kitty now.

"They must have done. Of course our bodies were never found in the river, but that wouldn't have meant anything. Considering what else was going on at that time, trawling the river for proof of our drowning was nobody's top priority—except perhaps our families'."

"So anyone who might have come to rescue you just believed that you were dead," I said.

"Yes. Sadly I'm not much of a swimmer these days. My body doesn't work quite the way it used to."

"I guess that's why you're not swimming in the Miglio di Manarola right now," I said.

"Oh, is that today? I don't know how I forgot. I used to swim in the sea every morning here. But"—she shrugged her birdlike shoulders—"things change."

I felt a brief pang of sadness, that Kitty and I would never again play mermaids together in the water, as we'd once done. Even if she *could* still swim, did eighty-six-year-olds even like playing mermaids?

But it didn't matter, really. What mattered was that we were together. And even if we weren't mermaids anymore, we would be something else.

"We escaped nearly eight weeks after you time traveled," Kitty went on. "I'd honestly thought I was going to go mad from isolation, but then we got lucky. A bomb exploded just down the road from where we were being held."

"That doesn't sound lucky!" I said.

"Well, it was, because in the chaos surrounding the attack, your father and I fled. We didn't know where we were, and we certainly didn't know where we were going, but we ran into the night and hoped for the best. The next day we worked out that we were in Wales, near Port Talbot. You know almost all the railway signs had been removed, or replaced with incorrect signs, to mislead any spies. If you didn't already know where you were—which we didn't—it was quite the struggle to work it out."

"So once you knew where you were," I said, "did you go home? Did you see your parents? And Justine and Thomas? What did they say? Who had been taking care of them? Had my mum come home?"

Kitty was shaking her head. "We couldn't go back to Bristol. It wasn't safe for us."

She explained that because their death statements had already been issued, everyone would have asked questions if they'd turned up alive. And the military would have been petrified that Kitty and my dad might tell people what had happened to them. She said that if they'd gone home, they would at best be taken away again, and at worst be killed. It wouldn't have just been unsafe for Kitty and Dad; it would have been unsafe for our whole families if they knew the truth. So Kitty never saw her parents again. They died in an air raid a few months later.

"I'm sorry," I told her.

"Thank you," she said quietly. "It's been years, of course. *Decades.* But I still miss them." She cleared her throat. "Fortunately I had your father to take care of me."

"If you couldn't go home, where *did* you go?" I asked.

"We managed to secure passage on a boat to Ireland."

"Why? What was in Ireland?" I asked.

"It was a neutral nation," Kitty explained. "It had sided with neither the Allied Forces nor the Axis Powers, so it seemed the safest place for us. Certainly safer than anywhere in England or Wales. We rented a flat in Cork, and your father found a job as a custodian to pay our bills, and we told everyone I was his daughter."

"A *custodian*?" I giggled. I'd rarely known my father to clean anything.

Kitty giggled a little, too, and even though she looked so old, her laughter sounded the same as I remembered. "He was a far better physicist than he was a custodian,

297

I'll tell you that! But there was a war on. We did what we must. He went by the name Robert Blair, and we told everyone that I was his daughter, Catherine Blair, and my mum had passed away. After a while, those just became our names, and our identities."

"If you pretend to be someone for long enough, then it doesn't even feel like pretending anymore," I said.

"Quite right. Your father never stopped studying time travel, though. Both because he had already devoted so much of his life to it, and also because he deeply, deeply hoped that he would be able to find out where you had gone."

"He never did figure out how time travel worked, though, did he?" I said. "All those years and close calls, and he never figured it out."

"No," Kitty agreed. "He didn't." She coughed into a handkerchief, then looked back up at me. "But I did."

CHAPTER 36

I stared at Kitty. Silently, she stared back. "*You* figured out the secrets of time travel?" I asked.

"Yes."

"How on earth did you do that?! Kitty—*you know how time travel works?*"

"Yes," she said again. Delicately she took a sip of water.

"So?" I poked her arm. "How does it work?"

She shook her head. "I'm not going to tell you."

"Oh, come on." I nudged her with my shoulder, but perhaps harder than I should have, and I saw her wince. I'd briefly forgotten how old Kitty was. I'd remembered only that she was Kitty.

"No," she said again.

"Oh, come on, you know I won't tell anybody. When have I ever not kept a secret for you?" I asked.

"That's not it. I trust you completely. But I won't tell you how time travel works. Not because *you* shouldn't know, but because I don't believe that *people* should know. There's a reason why time travel isn't part of our everyday experience. It's dangerous."

She told me that it's one thing when a portal appears randomly. That's a natural act, like a volcanic eruption or an earthquake. But when humans create portals of their own, it would be like creating an earthquake just to further your own goals. It's disturbing the natural order of things.

She went on, "I can understand why Intelligence suspected that your father understood time travel and was just refusing to tell them how it worked. If he had known, I imagine he *would* have kept that secret from them."

"So you understand how time travel works, but you've never actually done it yourself," I said.

"Correct."

Which meant that I was still the only person I knew— maybe the only person in the whole world—to have leapt through the years. "You *used* to want to," I reminded her. "You used to want to go on an adventure."

"And I have done," Kitty said. "I've traveled all over the world. I've met fascinating people everywhere I've gone. I've fallen in love—more than once—and sailed across the Atlantic Ocean and experienced nearly nine decades of innovation. I've led a life filled with adventure. I didn't need to time travel to do that."

Kitty told me that as the years passed, Dad brought her in on his research more and more. When she was at school in Ireland and he was working, it was a casual apprenticeship, similar to the sort of chores she did for him while they were held captive in Wales. But after the war ended, he became increasingly insistent that Kitty learn everything he knew.

"'I am so close,' he kept saying—for *years* he said how close he was," Kitty said. "And eventually, when he was around sixty years old, he admitted to me that he was concerned he might die before he had worked it all out, and he needed to be certain that I knew everything he knew, so that I could take over his work if the need arose."

"And did you need to?" I asked, my chest tight.

"Yes. Your father passed away in 1962. From natural causes, Lottie—a heart attack. I'm sorry."

I shook my head and wiped my eyes with the back of my hand. "You don't need to be sorry. I already knew he'd died. And actually, I'm *happy*. I'm so happy to hear that he died from a heart attack and not from the war, that he lived more than twenty years longer than I thought he had. And that he could kind of be *your* dad for all that time."

"He was," Kitty confirmed. "I was very lucky to have him. I don't know what I would have done otherwise."

"You would have figured it out," I told her. "If you'd been a ten-year-old girl all alone in the world, I promise, you would have figured it out. And I think he was lucky to have you, too. He didn't have any of his kids or his wife or anyone anymore. Really he just had you."

"And I believe that's why he chose me to be his apprentice, the repository for all his research. Or maybe he saw an innate problem-solving talent in me and wanted to cultivate that. I don't know. But he told me that he *needed* me to continue his work. That it was extremely important. Because . . ."

She coughed again, for longer this time. I held out her glass of water, but she waved it away.

"Do you remember your father's saying about coincidences?" Kitty asked once her throat was clear.

"Of course. 'When something seems like an unbelievable coincidence, then consider that it might not *be* a coincidence.'"

Kitty beamed at me. "*Exactly.* Well, that's what your father thought was the explanation for the portal that you went through."

"He thought it was an unbelievable coincidence?" I said.

"He thought that it was not, in fact, a coincidence."

"Like, it was too convenient for a portal to open up at the exact time that I needed to escape?"

Now that I'd said it, I realized that my dad had a point there. Most people went their whole lives without ever seeing a portal. How incredibly low *were* the odds that I would not only see one—but that I would see it three seconds before a bullet hit me?

"But if it was so convenient," I said slowly, "then why couldn't you come through the portal with me? Why would it be such a great coincidence for me, and such a useless one for you? That doesn't seem fair. It's never, ever seemed fair."

"It didn't seem fair to me at first, either," Kitty said. "I was glad you got out, but I was jealous that you got to time travel when you hadn't even wanted it, really, and I had. I didn't understand why you hadn't taken me with you—or sometimes, why I hadn't gone *instead* of you. There were times—especially when I was a teenager, living undercover in a strange country, hiding my identity—when I felt angry with you for abandoning me."

"I'm so sorry," I told her. "I have been sorry this whole time. I wish I'd brought you with me."

"I don't," she said. "Not anymore. I needed to stay there, in that facility, with your father. I needed to live by his side for the next twenty-two years. I needed to learn everything he had to teach me about time travel. Because eventually he came up with a theory: that the reason why a portal appeared in the exact time and place where you needed it was because either he or I, at some point in the future, would create it for you."

I felt like time stopped around us.

"What are you saying?" I whispered. "That the portal wasn't random at all?"

"Exactly."

"You're telling me that somebody created it, at some point in the future, and sent it back there to rescue me."

"Yes."

"And that somebody . . . that was you?"

"Yes," said Kitty again. "That was me."

CHAPTER 37

I was sobbing in Kitty's arms. "Thank you," I wept into her shoulder. "Thank you, thank you, thank you."

"Lottie, my darling, you don't need to cry. You don't even need to thank me. Rescuing you was the guiding reason for almost everything I've done over the years. I should be thanking *you* for somehow tracking me down and showing me that my life's work paid off. That I really did save you."

Still my tears kept coming. "I just felt so *guilty*," I told her. "Ever since I got to America, I've carried around this guilt, because *I left you to die*. And then when I saw that postcard, and I realized that you didn't die, that it wasn't my fault—I felt a million pounds lighter. And *now*, to learn that you couldn't even have come with me in the first place, because if you had then neither of us would have gotten out . . ."

I shook my head. It was too enormous. I couldn't wrap my mind around it.

"What if something had gone wrong, though?" I asked. "Like, what if my dad died before he was able to teach you everything he knew? What if you'd just never been able to figure out how to create the portal that I needed?"

"I worried about that," Kitty said. "By the time I finally created your portal, it was 2002. For years I'd feared that some terrible accident would befall me before I had the opportunity to complete my work.

"But your father never worried. He believed that time is . . . well, this is hard to explain to pretty much anyone who's not a theoretical physicist. But he believed—and I do, too—that time is not a straight line where first this happens and then the next thing happens and then the next. He believed that since the portal *did* show up for you in 1940, that meant that at some point in the future, somebody had *already* created it."

I was distracted enough by trying to understand this that my tears had stopped. "I don't get it," I said. "I mean, I sort of do, but when I try to focus in on exactly how it would work, it seems to crumble into little pieces."

"I've had more than seventy years longer than you to puzzle this one out," Kitty pointed out gently. "It doesn't need to make sense right away. I'm going to give you some of my research. Not all of it, but a few of the key pieces. I'm sure most of it will seem nonsensical at this point, but you can hold on to it. And maybe once you've graduated from college, or graduate school, or whatever it is you go on to do, you'll find some value in my notes."

She stood and walked slowly across the room to a credenza with silver candlesticks and china plates displayed behind its glass front. She bent over, deliberately, painfully.

"Can I help you?" I asked, already on my feet.

"No, no, that's fine. Goodness, I should be able to get around my own house by myself!" Finally she opened the cabinet doors below the glass front, and instead of seeing more dining room supplies, I saw that the bottom of the credenza was a filing cabinet stuffed with papers. Kitty started pulling out files. "You can have this one," she said, "and this one. . . . Oh, you'll definitely want this. . . . Now, where did I put the notes from the Paris meeting? . . ."

"Are you sure you want me to have all of this?" I asked, watching the piles of papers grow at her feet.

"I'm certainly not going to do anything else with it. My research on time travel stopped in 2002. Once I'd created your portal, my work was complete."

"Is it okay if I show all this to someone else?" I asked. "My friend Jake is really interested in all this stuff. He's the only person who knows where I really came from."

"Certainly." Kitty stopped pulling files and looked at me. "Jake. . . . Now, is he a friend who's a boy, or a boyfriend?"

"*Kitty*," I said in a withering tone. "Seriously?"

She laughed. "Do you remember when we had that crush on one of Justine's boyfriends? What was his name? The tall one, with the long eyelashes."

I started laughing, too. "Henry! Henry Lee."

"Oh, of course! How could I forget Henry Lee? And I dared you to write him a love letter."

"And I dared *you* to kiss him," I said.

"And then Justine threw her shoes at us!"

"She had terrible aim," I said.

"I wonder whatever happened to Henry Lee," Kitty mused.

"Who knows. That was the last time I ever saw him. I don't think he came around to call on Justine after all that."

"It's magical," Kitty said, "to have someone who remembers the same things I do."

"I know," I said. "It's even more magical than time travel."

I piled Kitty's files onto her coffee table, and then she took me out the back door of her house, so I could see the garden she kept there: flowers of all colors, and small lemon and orange trees. Butterflies darted among the plants, and the air smelled sweet and fresh.

"Since when do you garden?" I asked.

"Since I settled in Manarola. I spent so many years of my life on the run, or exploring the world, wandering from place to place. Once I had a home of my own, I wanted to make it feel permanent."

As I smelled her flowers, she told me that she'd moved here in 1987 because it seemed beautiful, remote, and, most importantly, safe—someplace no one would ever expect her to be. She was never confident that the British government had stopped looking for her. She never stopped worrying that if they *were* to find her, they would try to silence her.

"When I moved here," she said, "naturally I told everyone my name was Catherine Blair, and by now my Italian accent sounds almost like a native's."

"Impressive. I can't speak any other language. But I can mostly do an American accent."

"Yes, I noticed that," Kitty said drily. "Not my favorite of the world's accents, alas, but you carry it well."

"Did you ever have kids, or get married?" I asked her. "Was Ron Alama a code name for your husband?"

Kitty laughed with surprise. "Ron Alama? How did you even hear of him?"

"I read one of his papers," I told her. "And I figured out that it was your way of telling me to go to Manarola."

"Lottie, I think you're cleverer than I am. I *did* invent the name Ron Alama as an anagram of Manarola, but that was just for my own amusement, not because I ever once suspected you would be alive to find that name and piece together what it signified. Ron Alama was my own code name, for my own scientific research. As I continued to research time travel, I made a few useful discoveries with more everyday applications."

"That was *you* who came up with a way to treat cancer?"

Kitty smiled and picked a low-hanging orange from one of her trees. "It was." She told me that the other scientists who she worked with directly obviously knew that she was a woman, but they respected her decision to publish her findings under a male pseudonym. One of her colleagues even gamely volunteered to be the "face" of Ron Alama, posing for that headshot I'd seen all over the Internet. What none of them knew was that, to Kitty, this radiation treatment was just a step along the way toward her ultimate goal of creating a time travel portal.

"That radiation treatment improved the quality of life for quite a number of people in hospitals all over the world. You may not know it to look at my little cottage here, but I made an awful lot of money from that discovery as well. Suffice it to say that I will be well cared-for no matter how much longer I live, and had I had any children—which I did not—they also would find all their needs financially provided for."

"So you're rich?" I asked.

"Well . . ." Kitty demurred.

"You are! You are a rich inventor. I love it. My best friend is a rich inventor who knows how time travel works. Of course."

I tore off the peel on the orange Kitty had picked, offered her half, and took the other half for myself. It smelled more like an orange than I'd ever known an orange could smell.

"Here's what I don't understand," I said. "You didn't know that I traveled to Sutton in 2013. You didn't create the name Ron Alama so that I could find you here. You didn't even put up the 'Wills Tower' sign for me?"

"I did not," Kitty said. "I just liked it as a name for my house because I'm up so high in the mountains here, looking out over everything—it's what I imagined living in Wills Tower might feel like."

"So why did you put that note in *A Little Princess* at the Sutton library? That's what I don't get."

"I have a theory," Kitty answered. "So, as I told you, I've never been to Sutton. I've never even been to Wisconsin. I don't really know why anybody would—sorry, Lottie."

"I'm not offended," I told her.

"The closest I've ever been was Chicago. And even then, it's probably been, gosh, twenty years since I was there? But I wonder if the Chicago Public Library's copy of *A Little Princess* might have somehow wound up in Sutton."

"It definitely could have," I told her. "Miss Timms—the librarian—told me that some of the books in our collection were handed down from the Chicago library. *A Little Princess* could have been one of them. But . . . why would you have put this note in there in the first place? If that wasn't supposed to be a clue telling me how to find you, then why bother?"

"Because I always put notes in copies of *A Little Princess.*"

"What? Really?"

"Yes. Every time I see the book, into it goes a postcard or a piece of stationery or some such. You remember: My parents always told me that you must leave a note."

"Are your notes always about me?"

"Yes. They're all more or less like the note you showed me a few minutes ago. Different stationery or postcards, sometimes slightly different wording, but that's the gist of every one of them.

"As I said, Lottie, I have traveled all over the world. I've been to more than a hundred countries on every continent except Antarctica. And I've put notes about you in every copy of *A Little Princess*, in every language, in every place where I found it."

"Why?"

"It was silly," Kitty said. "It wasn't scientific at all. Every rational part of my brain told me that you would have gone too far into the past or future for you to ever find one of these notes. But I kept leaving them anyway, just in case, because . . ." She smiled at me. "Because it was silly, but I had hope." She took my hand in hers, the orange juice on our fingers sticking them together. "I love you," she said simply.

"I will always love you," I said to Kitty.

Epilogue

Epilogue

"Do you want to see what my mom gave me yesterday?" Jake asked me.

"Sure." We were standing outside Sutton Middle School, waiting for the doors to open and the day to begin. It was December now, nearly four months after our trip to Italy, and so chilly that I could see our breath forming little clouds in the air as we talked.

Jake pulled a plastic figurine out of his wheelie backpack and held it up. "Awesome, right?"

I inspected it closely. It looked pretty much the same as Jake's other action figures—and he had hundreds of them, I knew now from all the times I'd hung out at his house. "It seems awesome," I agreed. "Who is it?"

"Starfox! He's an Eternal and he has superhuman strength and protective abilities. Like he can fall from a ten-story building and not even get hurt." Jake lifted the figure as if to demonstrate, then paused. "I don't want to test it, though. Just because it works in the comic books doesn't mean it's going to work on a plastic toy."

I laughed.

"What are you reading?" Jake asked, gesturing to the book in my hands.

"*A Monster Calls.*" I flipped it around so he could see the front cover.

"'By Patrick Ness,'" he read. He looked up at me. "Wow, you're already on the *N*s?"

"I'm skipping some of the books now," I explained. "I'm just doing the interesting-looking ones, so it goes faster. Well, I guess not *that* much faster, because there are a lot of interesting-looking ones."

The first thing Kitty did after I found her was to make a donation to the Sutton Public Library—a donation big enough to keep it open for years and years. I didn't know how to thank her enough, but she just said, "Lottie, that's what I made the money for."

I'd spent the rest of my summer break and the first couple weeks of September helping Miss Timms unpack all the books we'd boxed up, and quickly the library was looking as good as ever—maybe even more so, now that Miss Timms could afford to replace some of the older computers and armchairs.

Now, the school doors opened, and Jake and I joined the press of students trying to get in out of the cold.

"Charlotte!" I turned and saw Sydney hurrying toward me. "Is it okay if my dad drops me off at seven tonight instead of six? He has to work late."

"Sure!" We headed through the doors together.

Dakota had been true to her word: Our friendship was over. And with it went my friendship with Kianna, Gavin's phone calls, and a lot of other people who'd been part of my day-to-day life in Sutton. But not all of them.

Sydney and I still did a lot of the things I used to do with the whole group—we'd paint each other's nails whatever crazy colors and patterns we felt like, and gossip about who had crushes on whom, and go out to the movies. Sydney kept hanging out with our old friends, too. Unlike Dakota, she didn't think she had to choose one or the other.

"Do you know what your grandmother's making for dinner?" Sydney went on. "I am *obsessed* with her cooking."

After funding the library, the second thing Kitty did was leave Manarola and move to Sutton.

"Are you sure?" I'd asked her. "It's so beautiful where you live, and Sutton is so . . . well . . ."

"American," Kitty supplied. "I know. But I've stayed more than long enough in Italy. I've let myself grow comfortable there. There's still time in my life for at least one more adventure."

"Sutton's not exactly an *adventure*," I warned her.

"Everything you and I do together is an adventure," she told me. And that was true.

Kitty bought a modest house in Sutton, not too far from Melanie and Keith's, and she decorated it the same as she had her house in Manarola: filled with books, and artifacts from her travels. She started a small garden—no lemon or orange trees here, though, as she said the climate wasn't right. She cooked a lot, pasta and fish dishes that even Melanie and Keith admitted, with surprise, were much better than the Italian restaurant at the mall.

The people who knew me in Sutton, like Sydney and Miss Timms, were all enthralled by her, this petite old lady who spoke several languages and could tell stories from so many places and times. "What a cool grandma!" Melanie told me. Only Jake knew the truth about who Kitty really was to me.

As for Jake, we spent a lot of time together now. Everything in Sutton was different from Italy, but when we were together, it was almost like we were back there, in that beautiful, golden summer when all dreams seemed achievable. Often I would sit and read while Jake sketched, or we would plan out our imaginary next trips to other places in the world—or sometimes other times in history or other planets in the sky, since, as Jake said, you just never know.

That was my life, day after day. Then those days turned into weeks, and the weeks into months, and the months into seasons. And just like that, years went by.

I kept getting older. And of course Kitty did, too. Eventually she couldn't garden anymore, though she still liked to look at her flowers. It became hard for her to cook, and then it became hard for her to eat. When she couldn't walk around anymore, I moved her African masks and Mexican wall hangings and Russian lacquer boxes near her bed, so she could still be reminded of how far she had traveled and how much she had done.

When her doctor said it was only a matter of time, I sat by Kitty's bedside, reading books to myself and talking to her on the rare occasions when she was awake.

"I'm going to miss you," I said.

"Of course you will," she replied. "But I'll always be with you. Wherever you go, I'll be with you."

"I know you will," I said. "And wherever you go, I'll be with you."

She opened and closed her lips a few times, as if she was trying to say something.

"Do you need anything?" I asked. "I'll get you whatever you want."

"No," Kitty said. "Just stay with me before I go."

So I held her hand. And I stayed.

ACKNOWLEDGMENTS

I am overwhelmed with gratitude to everyone who helped me turn the dream of Lottie and Kitty's story into a reality.

I will never be able to say thank you enough to my editor, Tamra Tuller, for believing in this story, believing in me, and knowing just how to turn this into the book it was meant to be.

Thanks to the rest of the team at Chronicle, including Ginee Seo, Sally Kim, Lara Starr, Taylor Norman, Daria Harper, Claire Fletcher, Marie Oishi, Kayla Ferriera, and Vicky Walker for welcoming me into your family of authors and working so hard to make this book a success.

To Stephen Barbara, for your enthusiasm, ingenuity, and perseverance. You make me believe that any creative undertaking is possible, as long as I have you by my side.

To my aides in achieving historical British accuracy, including my language specialist Carol Mason; the Churchill War Rooms and Churchill Museum; and Juliet Gardiner's *The Children's War: The Second World War Through the Eyes of the Children of Britain.*

To the Mamas and the Papas, whose song "Once Was a Time I Thought" inspired this book's title.

To Allison Smith, for taking that first trip to Cinque Terre with me.

To Brian Pennington, for supporting me the entire time I was writing this.

To all the friends I made in Bristol, especially Usman Ahmed, who advised on the Britishisms, and Hannah Slarks.

To the Type A Retreat girls—Emily Heddleson, Lexa Hillyer, Lauren Oliver, Jess Rothenberg, Rebecca Serle, and Courtney Sheinmel. It was sitting by your sides that I wrote the first words of this novel—just as I have written so many other words in the years I've been lucky enough to know you.

To Kendra Levin, one of the best editors (and friends) I know, for helping me craft this plot from the very beginning.

To my father, Michael Sales, whose wisdom and love provided the inspiration for the character of Lottie's dad.

And to my mother, Amy Sales, because everything we do together is an adventure.

Book Club Discussion Guide

1. Lottie makes the life-changing decision to jump through the time travel portal. Why do you think Lottie doesn't even try to pull Kitty through with her? If you were in Lottie's place, what would you have done?

2. When she searches for people she knows on the Internet, Lottie has the startling experience of reading the obituaries of her family members and of her best friend. What kinds of revelations does Lottie have when reading these life snapshots? What questions do they raise for her? What does she particularly notice about Kitty's obituary? How is she affected by it?

3. The French saying "plus ça change, plus c'est la même chose" roughly translates to "the more things change, the more they stay the same." The author gives us an idea of Lottie's English

life in the 1940s at the beginning of the novel before switching the setting to the United States in 2013. Lottie copes with enormous changes as she is thrust into the future. However, some things remain stubbornly the same between the two settings. Describe what has changed, and what has not. Does the author offer any suggestions about how these norms can change?

4. "Ever so occasionally, you come to a moment when everything about you is tested. When you must decide, with one action, what kind of friend and person you want to be" (138). Lottie comes to a harsh conclusion about herself at the end of Chapter 15. Do you agree that her decision to jump through the time portal makes her a bad friend and person?

5. The longer Lottie stays in her new life, the more her new identity is forged. She begins to lose her accent and memories of the past. Was this an essential step in Lottie's survival in her new world, or is she actually losing something essential by letting go of her memories?

6. Lottie comes to a realization when she sees Jake with his family: that you can have a home-self and a school-self. Do you have different sides of yourself that you show at home, at school, or elsewhere? If you shut out one self for long enough, do you think you can lose that part of yourself?

7. One risk that Lottie faces when she travels to Italy is disappointment. She says, "'[I]t's easier not to get something when you'd never even hoped for it in the first place'" (244). Do you agree or disagree? Would Kitty agree with her friend?

8. "I was *Charlotte*, whoever that might turn out to be" (125). Often, the farther we travel from home, the better we can understand it—and ourselves. What greater understanding does Lottie gain about her former life and herself from traveling to the future?

9. Lottie is a voracious reader, devouring the town library's catalog starting from the letter A. The following is a catalog of the books listed in *Once Was a Time*:
  - *A Little Princess,* by Frances Hodgson Burnett
  - *The Wonderful Wizard of Oz,* by L. Frank Baum
  - *Skellig,* by David Almond
  - *The Baby-Sitters Club #4: Mary Anne Saves the Day,* by Ann M. Martin
  - *The Giver,* by Lois Lowry
  - *The Book Thief,* by Marcus Zusak
  - *Tuck Everlasting,* by Natalie Babbitt
  - *Peter and the Starcatchers,* by Dave Barry and Ridley Pearson
  - *Tales of a Fourth Grade Nothing,* by Judy Blume
  - *A Monster Calls,* by Patrick Ness

Read one or more of the books on Lottie's reading list. How do these books inform Lottie's education? That is, how do these books teach Lottie about her own life and influence the way she confronts challenges? Use specific examples in your discussion. What books have played a key part in your education?

LEILA SALES is the author of the young adult novels *Mostly Good Girls, Past Perfect, This Song Will Save Your Life,* and *Tonight the Streets Are Ours.* She grew up outside of Boston, Massachusetts, graduated with a degree in psychology from the University of Chicago, and now lives in Brooklyn, New York. Like the characters in *Once Was a Time,* Leila loves books, travel, imaginary games, and her friends. Learn more at LeilaSales.com, and follow her on Twitter at @LeilaSalesBooks.